AFTERSHOCKS

MARISA REICHARDT

MARISA REICHARDT

AFTER SHOCKS

AMULET BOOKS · NEW YORK

Cataloging-in-Publication Data has been applied for and may be obtained from the Library of Congress.

ISBN 978-1-4197-3917-0

Text copyright © 2020 Marisa Reichardt
Book design by Hana Anouk Nakamura

Published in 2020 by Amulet Books, an imprint of ABRAMS. All rights reserved. No portion of this book may be reproduced, stored in a retrieval system, or transmitted in any form or by any means, mechanical, electronic, photocopying, recording, or otherwise, without written permission from the publisher.

Printed and bound in U.S.A.
10 9 8 7 6 5 4 3 2 1

Amulet Books are available at special discounts when purchased in quantity for premiums and promotions as well as fundraising or educational use. Special editions can also be created to specification. For details, contact specialsales@abramsbooks.com or the address below.

Amulet Books® is a registered trademark of Harry N. Abrams, Inc.

ABRAMS The Art of Books
195 Broadway, New York, NY 10007
abramsbooks.com

To my mom—

For believing in me. Always.

DAY ONE

FRIDAY

CHAPTER ONE

4:15 P.M.

I'M SKIPPING PRACTICE.

Skipping practice isn't something people who want to play water polo in college should do, but sometimes you find out your mom is dating your coach and there is absolutely, positively no way you can show your face on the pool deck.

My mom broke the news to me last night at dinner. It was casual. Like, "Pass the peas and, oh yeah, Coach Sanchez is my new boyfriend."

I gagged. Literally. On a combination of food and disgust.

She ignored my disdain. "It's a good thing, Ruby. I promise." Her gaze floated to some faraway, blissful place. "We're actually going on a little romantic getaway for Valentine's Day next weekend."

Did she have to use the word *romantic*?

And did she have to swoon over *Valentine's Day*?

Since when does my mom believe in hearts and flowers? I want her to be happy. I do. But does she have to find happiness in my world? With *my* coach?

"That's it," I said. "I have to switch schools."

"Don't be so dramatic."

"This isn't dramatic, Mom. This is serious. You've ruined my life. So thanks a lot."

I pushed my chair away from the table and stormed off to my room, where I mainlined Netflix for the rest of the night, too horrified to tell anyone what I'd learned. I wasn't ready to tell my friends. Or my boyfriend. Maybe nobody would ever have to know.

But then the thoughts crept in.

What if they last forever?

What if my mom becomes Mrs. Coach Sanchez?

I wouldn't be able to keep it secret.

They'd have a sunset wedding on the beach, with me as the reluctant maid of honor. So different from the way my mom married my dad at city hall. And then Coach Sanchez would be in my living room on Sundays and on the couch on Christmas. In sweatpants with his whistle around his neck. A horrid visual. He belongs on the pool deck, not at my dinner table.

I don't dislike Coach Sanchez. I love him as my coach with his dorky jokes and his six-on-five plays and his surprise buñuelos after morning workouts. But in my house? With my mom? As my possible stepdad? No. My worlds were separate. Water polo was my happy place, home was my safe space. The two worlds colliding meant both were ruined.

Later in the night, after she spilled her news, my mom knocked on my door. Three gentle taps. Short and sweet.

"Ruby, can I come in?"

"Nope."

"Ruby."

I heard the thump of her pressing her forehead to the wood door as she sighed. I could feel her there even though I couldn't see her. And when I sensed she'd finally walked away, I cracked my door open. There she was, shuffling down the hall toward her bedroom, head bent. Defeated.

Good.

I wanted her to feel guilty. I wanted her to wallow in her selfishness and the way she had crossed the line. I hoped that's what she was thinking about as she fell asleep.

She was already gone for work when I left today, and I was glad I didn't have to see her. We had a late-start so we didn't have morning practice. But I saw Coach in the hallway as soon as I got to school because he also teaches chemistry. I couldn't look him in the face. Did he know my mom had told me? How long had they been a thing? I tried to figure out what clues I had about them as I unloaded my books into my locker. I remembered the way they'd been talking, heads tilted toward each other, shoulders touching, when I came out of the locker room after my game last week. I was worried my mom had been doing something inappropriate, like asking Coach why he'd benched me for practically the whole fourth quarter. *Because I need you to try smarter, not harder*, he'd told me. I hadn't imagined they were making plans for Valentine's Day.

Shudder.

Because it was a late-start day, Thea, Iris, and Juliette had insisted we meet up with Mila for breakfast even though Mila and I were barely on speaking terms since our New Year's Eve meltdown five weeks ago. When I'd gotten up the guts to tell the four of them about my mom and Coach, I was hoping for support, but Mila rolled her eyes because that's what she does best. "Guess we all know who'll be the star player now. Red-carpet rollout for you from the locker room to the water. Should I ready my camera? Go full-blown paparazzi on your ass?"

Mila's great at water polo. And sarcasm.

"Try the opposite," I said. "Coach will probably be extra tough on me now. Like he has to prove a point he's not playing favorites."

Mila slowly stirred her yogurt. "I wouldn't count on it. You're basically his favorite already. Now maybe we know why."

Damn. She knew how to aim.

Thea, Iris, and Juliette nodded their heads in agreement because that's what people who aren't me do with Mila. Smile. Nod. Repeat.

There was no way I could go to afternoon practice after that. Not when I knew Mila would spend the whole day texting the rest of the team to tell them Coach was making out with my mom and treating me like royalty.

So I skipped.

And now I'm here.

At the laundromat.

For one reason and one reason only: it's next door to the liquor store, and Mila taught me this is where you go when you need someone to buy you beer. There's always a surfer or a burnout or a sailor from the navy base practically waiting to be asked. There's a party tonight, and it seems like the perfect place to drown my sorrows or whatever it is you're supposed to do when you find out your coach likes to stick his tongue in your mom's mouth.

Ew. No!

I pound at my skull, trying to erase the visual. Beer will help. Even if I swore I'd never get beer this way after what happened the last time. But that was before I knew there would be a day like this. I'm taking a cue from Mila, and I don't even care if it makes me a hypocrite.

I dump an armful of beach towels into a washer and scope things out. There's an older woman folding laundry in a cubby in the back corner. She works here, and customers pay her to do their laundry. There's also a guy who doesn't look much older than me, but right now he's my only option. I push a bunch of quarters into the washer's slot and listen to the swoosh of water filling the drum as I try to figure out exactly how I'm going to work up the nerve to ask this prep in a polo to take my money and buy me a twelve-pack. If Mila were here, she'd do her usual skirt-and-flirt routine. Me? I'm six feet tall. This makes me great at playing the two-meter position in water polo but not so great at finding skirts that end past the crotch of my underwear. So I'm in jeans. And my team sweatshirt. With my feet shoved into flip-flops so well worn, the toe impressions are permanently carved into them. If asking people to buy you beer were covered on the SAT, I'd ace it. But it's not. So I'm nervous.

I watch the guy's hands as they carefully smooth over the folds of T-shirts and khaki pants with the precision of an assembly line.

One day I will meet someone with bigger hands than mine.

I notice stray blue paint on his knuckles. A little more under his chin. He piles his folded shirts into a duffel bag similar to the one I have for water polo, only his bag is hand-dyed like an art project, his name spray-painted in black stenciled letters along the side.

C. Smith.

He could be anyone.

C. Smith is so common that he is nameless. C. Smith is a face in the crowd. There are probably at least twenty C. Smiths in this town alone, two of them in my graduating class.

He finishes folding and pulls out a journal from his unzipped duffel. I try not to roll my eyes. He's probably one of those writer types who has to jot down everything he sees so he can shove it into a metaphor in some future story. His journal is black with the same letters stenciled in gold across the front. *C. Smith.* He opens up to a half-filled page and writes something inside. Then he closes the journal and tucks the ballpoint pen into an elastic band that wraps around the outside.

I fish my phone out of my back pocket and snap a photo of my washing machine suds to send to Leo while I'm thinking up a plan.

I watch the triple dots bounce as he types back to me.

What is that???

I don't respond because C. Smith abandons his duffel bag to wander the lavender-scented fluffy air of the laundromat, his casual cool in conflict with his perfect khaki pants. The older woman folding laundry in the back corner looks up when he moves—a quick intake of who's here and where they're going. My gaze skims across the timer on C. Smith's dryer, my stomach twisting with urgency when I realize I have only ten minutes left to summon up the courage to get what I came for.

I watch as he balances between his heels and the balls of his feet, checking out the flyers on the bulletin board. Winter sun shimmers through the open door next to him, shooting sparks across the checkered floor streaked with sticky gray stains and shreds of mop strings pushed into the corners. He must not care about the phone number for the woman opening up her house to align people's chakras on Saturday morning because he turns away to lean his back against a floor-to-ceiling window that frames the cracked asphalt and faded lines of the parking lot. He pushes his hand through his crew cut, and I notice that some of the strands in front are sun faded and nearly white.

I tug on the strings of my sweatshirt hood to bury my face and hide my lurking.

There's something oddly satisfying about watching someone when they don't know you're looking. To be making plans they'll be involved in but don't even know yet.

C. Smith crosses his arms over his chest. The sleeves of his shirt ride up to hug buff biceps, and I wonder if he started lifting weights recently or if, like me, he did weight-room workouts for four years of high school, jolting awake to an alarm clock for sports practice before the sun came up.

Six minutes on his dryer. It's now or never. I take the last sip of the bottled water I brought with me. It goes down too fast and I cough. C. Smith looks my way, acknowledging my presence with a lift of his chin.

I push my stool back and stand up, nervously spinning my championship ring around my finger and back again. Now that I'm standing, I can see I tower over C. Smith. I estimate he barely hits five feet and five inches.

So I slouch.

I would love to be five foot five.

I would love to not stand out.

I would love to be a nameless face in the crowd.

C. Smith has it good.

Or maybe he doesn't.

Short boys might not have it any better than tall girls.

"Excuse me." I take a step closer to him.

C. Smith lifts his eyes my way. "Yeah?"

A dog barks in the distance. It's a little yip at first, but then it gets frantic enough to make us both look out the window.

"I was wondering if you could do me a favor."

Dogs up and down the block join the barking in a wild cacophony of noise.

Like a warning.

Exactly as I process this thought, the ground rumbles underneath my feet. An empty laundry cart teeters by on its rickety wheels. C. Smith steps away from the window and braces his hands on top of the thick mint-green Formica table a few feet from mine, his neat shirts stacked in his duffel bag inches from his fingers.

We lock eyes.

"Earthquake," I say.

"Yeah. It feels big."

I nod. He's right. This one is bigger than normal. I grip the edge of my table, my fingertips flinching at the rotted bumps of dried gum underneath.

My water bottle bounces to the ground as the alarms of parked cars bleat. An open dryer door bangs with so much force its glass window breaks. C. Smith has his back to the laundromat's window. I'm facing it, looking out at the ground swelling in the parking lot.

And then there's a sound like a freight train.

Screeching.

Grinding.

The ground rolls like waves in the ocean. My knuckles go white as I struggle to hang on to the edge of my table.

A flash of movement catches my eye as the woman from the back corner darts out from her workspace, her hands flipping switches on a nearby panel. Washers and dryers stop midcycle. The fluorescent lights above us sputter then shut off as she runs out the door and into the parking lot.

She should not run into the parking lot.

I want to yell at her. Tell her to stop. Turn around. How can one person be so smart and so dumb at the same time?

C. Smith tries to get my attention, yelling incoherent words and waving his arms.

"Duck!" I shout, and dive under my own table in time to see the walls of the building cave in. The windows shatter. Fragments of glass slide across the floor like ice.

I grew up in California and can count on my fingers the number of times an earthquake had actually felt strong enough to make me run for cover. There was one time in kindergarten when Ms. Curtis was reading a story out loud from her big yellow book, and the ABC rug felt like it was going to drop out from under us. She told us to get underneath our desks and put one hand over our heads while holding on to a desk leg with the other. Ms. Curtis scrunched up like a pill bug in the middle of the room, showing us what to do before she rolled up under her own desk. Amanda Friedlander cried and Scotty Cleary peed his pants. I stayed curled up in a ball until the ground stopped shaking.

But then it was over. And just like that, the panic had passed. Nothing was broken. And Ms. Curtis went back to reading.

When I was in second grade, the earth must've rattled hard enough to scare my mom because she pulled me out of bed in the middle of the night and dove underneath the dining room table, where I stayed safely tucked against her chest until the ground stilled.

There was another time in middle school. And one more in tenth grade. When I was with Mila. Before everything.

Four times.

Four times in my seventeen years that I've ducked for cover because I actually thought my California town had the potential to split open.

Now it's actually happening.

The air explodes with scraping metal. The doorway caves. Drywall dust thickens like smoke. Chunks of ceiling debris fall and scatter. The table above me cracks and dips in the middle, pinning me down. Locking me in. I push against it, trying to keep it from collapsing and crushing me, but this earthquake is stronger than I am. I clench my eyes shut, ball my fists. I remember what I can. Cover my head. Tuck in my toes. Keep cuts to a minimum. The weight on my chest grows, stunting my breathing. I dare to squint my eyes open, but I can't see through the smog of chaos. I can't even pull enough breath into my lungs to scream.

Today will be the end of me.

The ground shakes. The walls fall.

People don't survive buildings collapsing on them. I'm going to die in a dirty laundromat, decorated all orange and green like a 1970s prom, and my mom won't know where to look for my body because she doesn't even know I'm here. I should be at the pool. With my team. With her boyfriend.

I'd give anything to be there now.

Instead of with C. Smith.

Who has disappeared.

Is he even alive? Did he duck when I warned him?

He was so close to the window. He could've been shredded apart by shards of glass. I scream. I don't know if it's for him or for me. My voice isn't loud enough. And my head isn't clear enough to know.

Heavy things drop. Shift. Move.

Walls and windows blow out.

The building rains down around me.

A boom.

A screech.

A bump.

A roll.

And just as quickly as it had started moving, the earth takes a final gasp. Its waves slow like it is out of breath.

Until finally, stillness.

CHAPTER TWO

4:40 P.M.

I COUGH THROUGH THE DUST.

Wiggle my body.

Flick my toes.

Roll my neck.

I've ended up sort of on my right side, sort of on my back, with my forearms crisscrossed over my face. I've got one fist on top of my head and another one trying desperately to keep a grip on the leg of the table above me. There's solid floor underneath me, but the walls of the building have buckled, surrounding me in rubble. Air strains in from a tiny slice in the debris, bringing a gift of light. The heat of my exhale presses back against my mouth. There's no room for my breath to move. It's trapped like me. I try to squirm. Scramble. Twist. But I barely budge.

There's nowhere to go.

No way out.

My heart beats so wildly I half expect it to stop.

A person's heart isn't meant to beat this fast.

I scream and scratch at the sliver of light, desperate to make it bigger. Dirt and dust and rocky bits of building drop down around me. I have to slow down. The rubble is unstable. Digging is dangerous. I know this. I've been taught this.

But I need air.

I'm suffocating.

I swipe my face clean and cinch the hood of my sweatshirt over my eyes to protect them. I claw at the hole in a panic. Drywall dust lodges underneath my fingernails but I manage to make a big enough space for real air to enter. I inhale deeply, my lungs expanding with the relief of oxygen even though I need to cough out the grime and dirt that comes with it. I'm probably choking on asbestos.

Then I feel the pain. A searing ache along the left side of my head above my ear. Surely I'm dying.

I reach for the wound. Press against it. Will the ache to stop. And then someone is wailing and I'm not alone. The cry is primal. It is fear. It is agony. It is close. But muffled. Buried, too.

"C. Smith?!" I yell. "Are you there? Is that you?"

He grunts. "There's something—on me. It's heavy." Another grunt. "Can't—breathe."

There's the scrape of metal against metal. A groan. I picture toppled triple-load washing machines crushing his small frame.

"What are you doing?!" I shout.

"I'm just—I need to get this off me."

"What is it? Can you move? Can you crawl out from under it?" I hear the rise in my voice. The frantic sound of it. The plead. The beg. "You have to move. You have to find air."

"I'm—trying."

Another push. Another screech of metal. Another grunt. And then silence. I wait in it. I wade in it. Tentatively whispering his name.

"C. Smith?"

I'm scared to ask because I'm scared of no answer. When I finally hear him suck in a breath, I flood my own lungs with air. With relief. I'm so grateful to know I'm not here alone. Even though I shouldn't wish this nightmare on anybody else.

"Where are you?" he says.

"I don't know. Trapped. Where are you?"

"I went under the table across from yours but I didn't get all the way under it."

"But you have air?"

"I do now." He moans. "Barely."

"Are you okay? How bad are you hurt?"

"I don't know."

"What does that mean?"

"There was something on me. On my chest. I moved it but I don't know. I just—I don't know."

"You're going to be okay." I say this firmly. With conviction. He has to believe me so I can believe me.

I remember having the stomach flu for the first time as a kid. I felt like leftovers gone bad in the fridge. I told my mom I was dying.

"You're not," she said, gently dabbing a cold wet washcloth across my sweaty forehead. "Your body knows how to recover. You just have to get through this."

"We just have to get through this," I tell him. I tell myself. I hear my mom's voice: *Ruby Babcock, you just have to get through this.*

Outside, sirens wail. Car alarms. Fire alarms. And then a cough from C. Smith right here and now. He's only a few feet from me. The place got tossed, but he's close. I spread my fingers out above my head, trying to make contact. Like feeling the physical skin-and-bones presence of him will make me feel less alone. He coughs again and I pull my hand back. What if he's dying?

"Do you have air? Can you breathe?" he says.

"I can." But for how long? And is this table teetering? What is that creaking sound? Is it only a matter of time before the legs break and the unstable walls of this tiny safe space collapse on top of me? Panic spirals to my fingers and toes. It shortens my breath. I focus on anything else.

"What's your name?" I can't keep calling him C. Smith.

A push. A hiss. "Charleston."

"Like the dance?"

"Like the city. When your last name's Smith, your parents are pretty much obligated to give you a bold first name." A grunt.

"My friends call me Charlie, though. Because Charleston makes me sound like an asshole."

"Are you *from* Charleston?"

"Conceived there."

"That's . . . graphic."

"No kidding. I can't even think of Charleston without imagining my parents boning."

He actually manages a laugh. It's pained but legitimate. His laugh makes me laugh.

"I shouldn't be laughing," I say.

"I'm glad you're laughing. It's making me laugh and—" A groan. "I'd rather die laughing."

"You're not going to die."

"Okay." A grunt. "Do you have a name?"

"Ruby."

"Ruby? Were you conceived at a fifties-themed restaurant made famous for its cheeseburgers?"

Another laugh escapes. "Ruby's Diner? No."

"Ruby's the name of my dog. Is that weird?"

"I don't know. Is it?"

"I guess not."

I can feel the stiffness settling. In my shoulders. In my legs. Reminding me how stuck I am. I want to spread out but I can't. My hands are over my head with only a couple inches of space all around me. I pat the ground under my head, and the cracked, teetering table above it. There are shards of glass and things split in half. I sense how tight things are. How small. I have no room. My heart races.

This is a coffin.

I suck in air.

Flap my hands as much as I can.

"Someone has to find us soon," I say.

Surely first responders are already responding. Firefighters. Rescue workers. I can hear the sirens on top of the car alarms. So much noise. They'll be here. Because there isn't enough air. There isn't enough room. There isn't anything but a pain in my head and Charlie trying to catch his breath.

Tears track through the dust on my face. Then I gasp. Choke on a sob.

"Ruby? Ruby, what's wrong?" Charlie's voice rises in panic.

I squeeze my eyes shut. "I want my mom." I feel bad for getting so mad at her last night. "I can't breathe."

"Ruby! Listen to me. It's going to be okay." Charlie's voice cuts through the stillness. It is strong. Sure. Like someone who has been trained for situations like this. "It's going to be okay."

"How do you know that?"

"Because you said so!"

What do I know? Growing up in California doesn't make me an earthquake expert. And what if the whole world looks like this laundromat? This could be the end of everything. I push at the pain in my head. It's still there. Throbbing.

"We should make noise," I say. "We need to scream so someone will hear us."

Charlie lets out a low and guttural yell. I follow with a scream, high and screeched. I scream over Charlie, through the rubble and out into the dusty air, until my throat hurts and my chest heaves and my head feels like it could explode.

Someone will hear us. Someone will help.

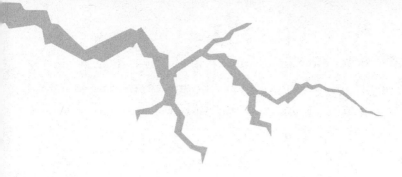

CHAPTER THREE

5:00 P.M.

THROUGH THE PAIN AND THE DUST AND THE dirt, a speck of a promise slips through.

"Charlie! My phone!"

"Get it!"

I hear the hope in his voice and suddenly wish I'd kept the revelation to myself. Because okay, fine, I have a phone, but, "It's in my back pocket and I can't move my arms. Where's yours?"

"Hell if I know. We need yours. Okay?"

"Okay." I coax my left arm off my face, but the space above me is tight, pushing down. Boxing me in. My arm, just below my elbow, scrapes against a sharp slice of something jutting out from overhead. Glass, I think. From the window. A jagged spike rips through the sleeve of my sweatshirt and into my flesh like the tip of a knife cutting through birthday cake. Up and down my forearm the shock goes, like it's cut clean through my skin and tissue and gone straight to the bone. The pain sears through me and I cry out.

"What is it? What happened?"

I grit my teeth, biting down to get through the burning pain. My vision fades for a split second, making everything too bright, like a camera flash. My stomach rolls with nausea. Then just as quickly, I'm back in the dark and panting again. I can't twist my body enough to see the damage, but I can feel the blood as it spills out and seeps into the thick cotton sleeve of my sweatshirt.

"What happened?!" Charlie shouts this time. "Answer me!"

My stomach lurches again. I might throw up. I heave.

"Ruby!"

"I cut myself. I think it's bad." I'm scared to touch it. I don't want to feel how deep it is. I don't want to feel my own muscle and bone.

Charlie's voice rises again. "Get your phone. We need help."

"I'm close but I can't." I whimper. "I can't get it."

"Ruby. Focus." Every time Charlie says my name, it grounds me. "There's literally nothing more important right now."

I twist my body into the inches of give this space will allow me, finally managing to get the tips of my left fingers into my back pocket. "Wait!" I can feel it. "I've almost got it." I push my fingers a millimeter deeper, but I can't pull it free. "I'm trying."

"Don't give up, Ruby."

My arm screams with pain, a sharp spike carving, but the extra push is enough to get my hand all the way into my pocket.

I pull my arm back, crying out as the spike cuts back through the other way. "I have it!" I shove my phone so close to my face that I can't even see the whole thing at once. Blood drips down my hand and smears the screen. I try to wipe it clean with my chin. "It's five o'clock."

"Who cares what time it is? Do you have any reception?"

I swipe at my phone and dial 9-1-1. When I press the green call button, my phone sits there, doing nothing, not paying attention to me. Like a glazed-over Leo playing video games last summer on the massive sectional couch in Michael Franklin's pool house while Mila and I texted annoyed sighs back and forth across the room.

Mila doesn't text me anymore.

"Nothing's happening," I say.

"What are you trying to do?"

"I dialed nine-one-one."

"Everyone's doing that. Try something else."

Right. What was I even thinking? The 9-1-1 lines have to be crammed. "I'll call my mom." I pull up her number and press the green call button again. And there is . . . nothing. "It's not going through."

"Try again."

I do. Still nothing. "I can't." It feels like my failure. Like it's my fault my phone doesn't work after an earthquake. I never should've told Charlie I had it. I never should've given him hope.

"Crap!" He punches something and I wait, frozen, as the space around us creeks and sways. Charlie sucks in a breath. "Oof."

"What's wrong?"

"I hurt."

"Where?"

"Everywhere. My ribs hate me."

I don't like knowing Charlie's in pain. "But your head's fine. You aren't concussed?"

"*Concussed?* Why wouldn't you just call it a concussion?"

"Argh. I don't know." It's a term they used in this junior life-guard program I did as a kid. I was super obsessed with calling everything by the correct name because I wanted the instructors to see my dedication. So they would think I was the best. I don't even know what I'm saying right now. "Just—are you okay? Do you have a head injury?"

"I don't think so. Everything fell on my chest. I saw you put your hand over your head so I did the same thing." He groans.

My own head hurts enough for me to have a possible concussion. Or a brain bleed. Is a brain bleed the same thing as a concussion? It's likely either one could kill me. Is it a painful death? Or will I simply fall asleep and not wake up?

Wait. What if I fall asleep and don't wake up?

"Is your head okay, Ruby?"

"I don't know. It hurts." I press at the pain.

"How bad?"

"Bad. But not like my arm."

"Is it bleeding?"

"My arm or my head?"

"Both. Either. You tell me."

"My arm is bleeding. Underneath my elbow."

"Is it gushing blood?"

"More like oozing."

He coughs. "You should apply pressure to try to stop the bleeding."

Thinking about the seep of blood makes me light-headed. Foggy. If I could just shut my eyes for a second . . .

"Ruby!" Charlie's shout is an electric jolt of energy to my brain. "Can you get your arm out of your sweatshirt sleeve so you can wrap it around your cut and use it to apply pressure?"

"I'll try." I wiggle. I'm like a worm. No arms. No legs. Rolling a millimeter in either direction, trying to avoid every sharp thing as I ease my arm out of the sleeve. It feels like hours pass, but I finally get it. "It's off."

"Okay. You need to wrap as much of it as you can as tight as you can around your arm. But don't make it so tight that you cut off your circulation."

"Are you a Boy Scout?"

"Hell no."

I laugh, letting go of my worry long enough to free my right hand and wrap the sleeve around my left arm. I pull it tighter by using my teeth. I grunt through each step, all of it so much effort in this limited space.

"Got it."

"Good. Good job, Ruby."

A small laugh escapes my lips.

"What?"

"I don't know. I imagined you talking to your dog just then, like, *Good dog, Ruby.*"

"Well, Ruby would dig us the hell out of this mess, that's for damn sure."

"I wish Ruby was here."

"Me too."

"So now what?"

"We wait."

"For how long?"

"Who knows? Until it stops. Until we get help."

I feel like we're talking about two different things now. The bleeding and this nightmare.

"And then I can untie it?"

"When it stops, yes." He sounds so calm. Like someone trained to deliver bad news without any emotion. How did he get this way? "It'll be okay, Ruby. Now can you try your phone again?"

I pull my phone back to my face with my free hand. Press the redial button. Absolutely zero happens. "Nothing. It won't dial out."

"Text?"

I type out a text to my mom with my right thumb: *I'm trapped at the Suds and Surf laundromat on Belmont.* None of those words looks real.

My phone waits and waits and waits. "It won't go through."

"Can you get online?"

I try that. The swirly gray ball at the top of the screen whips around and around, struggling to load. It's hopeless. Everything is down. Everyone is unreachable.

No phone calls. No texts.

But then my phone dings with an emergency alert from the California Earthquake Warning System.

7.8-magnitude quake. 4:31 p.m. PST San Andreas fault line. Severe damage.

My vision blurs. All I see is *7.8-magnitude.*

My heart stops in my chest. I think of my house. Of my mom. My school. My friends. Are they okay?

"Charlie," I whisper. "It was a seven point eight."

"No."

"Yes."

"No."

The worst earthquake I've ever experienced was probably a high magnitude 4, and it barely broke a couple of glasses in our cupboard. So when you figure each additional point is something like thirty times more energy, I'm pretty sure a magnitude 7.8 is "The Big One."

Charlie's clearly done the same math.

"Can you try your phone again?" His voice sounds different. Like hope has left it. Reality has sunk in.

I call my mom again. Text her. Still nothing. I can only hope she's okay and she'll get my messages eventually. "I'll keep trying."

Something suddenly pops. I flinch. Hit my head. Another pop. And another. Three times. Then a sizzle. The sound seems like it's coming from outside. Away from us, but still close enough to hear.

"What was that?" I say.

"My best guess would be a downed power line."

"It's outside, right?" I think of the toppled washing machines. The water that surely leaked out. This isn't a good place to be near downed power lines thrashing around like out-of-control garden hoses.

"Definitely outside. Pretend it's fireworks."

Fireworks. "I like fireworks." They remind me of the day I met Leo. I do what Charlie tells me. I close my eyes and pretend.

LEO

There's something about fireworks.

The crisp crackle of them equals a promise, and it's suddenly okay to wish on new beginnings. It's okay to wish on kisses from the boy you're sharing a towel with on a dark sandy beach on the Fourth of July while the bright lights wheeze their way upward to bust open the sky above.

Maybe I got caught up in the idea of fireworks on that night seven months ago when Leo weaved his way through the masses to plop down next to me, still smelling like sunblock at nine p.m.

We'd just met but had been flirting all day. A smile here. A touch there. By the afternoon, we were tangled feet under the ocean water. He was at least as tall as me and wore red-, white-, and blue-striped board shorts that were more subtle than cheesy.

"Summer," he said, leaning back on his elbows in the sand as the sun skimmed the horizon. "Doesn't it seem like everything lasts longer? A week feels like a year."

"So a day feels like a week?"

He looked at me. Squinted. "More like a month."

"So you've known me a month."

"Yeah." He smiled. Shy. "It's been a good month."

What he'd said was true. My arrival at the beach with Mila

at ten a.m. felt like weeks ago. Since then there had been body-surfing and volleyball and a bonfire. Lunch. Dinner. Multiple applications of sunblock. Beer.

All day long, Leo had been at my side, asking me questions and answering mine. He was funny and smart and thoughtful. And even though I was wearing a bikini, he looked at my eyes when he talked to me. It's sad how that's a thing you notice when you're a girl at the beach. I wondered how I hadn't talked to him before, but maybe it's because we weren't meant to talk until that day.

In the dark, a few hours later, waiting for fireworks, he handed me an unlit sparkler stick.

"Want me to light it?" he asked, nudging his broad swimmer's shoulder against mine.

"Yes. I want you to light me up." I'd intended to make a joke, but I realized how it sounded and wished I could disappear.

But Leo laughed.

"Just you wait, Babcock," he said, flicking a lighter open and holding the flame to the tip of my sparkler. The fire sizzled and swirled, shooting sparks into the air and onto the sand, where they instantly died. "Just you wait."

CHAPTER FOUR

6:18 P.M.

THERE ARE SIRENS OUTSIDE, THEIR SCREAMS slicing through the hollow holes of the laundromat. I angle my body toward them, like they'll sense my presence as they pass. My throat is caked with dust. Each inhale is dry and gritty. Filth gets stuck in my chest until it hurts, like breathing smog-filled air on a hot California day. I know it's impossible to hear my cries for help over the wail of the sirens, but I yell anyway because it's the only thing I can do.

"You can probably loosen your sweatshirt from your arm now," Charlie says when I pause to suck in air. "Just a little. See if the bleeding has stopped."

I've been trading off between my teeth and my right hand to pull the sweatshirt taut. My jaw is tight. My fingers are stiff. It's a relief to give them both a break. The pain isn't gone, but I don't feel any blood rushing to the surface when I let go.

"I think it's okay."

"Good. When we get out of here, we'll go to a nice hospital and get it all cleaned up just to be safe."

"A hospital? I don't want to go to a hospital." My heart races with panic. I hate hospitals. Hospitals are where people go to die. "I'm not going to the hospital."

"Fine. I won't force you."

Charlie drags in a labored breath then coughs. It's hard to ignore the fact that we don't have water. I'm lucky. I drank a water right before the earthquake. But I could easily down another gallon.

"When's the last time you had water, Charlie?"

"Lunchtime. Does your throat feel like you swallowed protein powder straight?"

"Worse." I know there's plenty of time before we have to start worrying about water but it's hard not to think about it when the air scratches my throat with every inhale.

I keep telling myself it's only a matter of time. That we won't have to wait much longer to be rescued. I tell myself this even though the sirens are spinning in the distance now. Away from here. Away from us.

I can guess where they are instead.

Downtown.

My mom's office.

Firefighters in heavy coats, brandishing flashlights and whistles while dogs pad their way across the concrete slabs, pressing their noses to the rubble of fallen buildings. I've only seen images like that on TV, happening in places far from home. Haiti. Mexico. Japan. Even though everyone thinks California is earthquake country, the temblors we have are mostly small. News coverage generally consists of a local reporter at a grocery store talking to a manager who's pointing out all the stuff that had fallen off the shelves. Even the Ridgecrest quake we had on the Fourth of July, which registered relatively big at a magnitude 7.1, didn't do a lot of damage. I was at the beach with Leo, where I'd felt nothing, but my mom was home and said it had only made our shutters sway.

The worst damage I'd seen was from Northridge, in 1994, when whole apartment buildings crumbled to the ground. Or San Francisco, in 1989, when the upper level of the bridge collapsed, crushing cars and people on the lower deck. But I wasn't alive then. Those earthquakes aren't a part of my history like they are for my mom. She remembers them. But to me, they're only pictures on the TV or online. And those earthquakes weren't The Big One. Even though The Big One is supposed to happen, even though I've grown up being told we're overdue and we should be ready for it to take place in my lifetime, the actual big earthquakes I've known have happened to other people. In other places. Far away from here.

I should've known better. Nothing is ever so far away that it's impossible.

I took an emergency earthquake kit to every first day of school from preschool through eighth grade, but the water bottles, thermal blanket, and seven-day supply of nutritional protein bars weren't real. The ground never shook hard enough for teachers to have to distribute them. Those kits were something I held in my hands for five minutes then handed to my teacher to stash away in the back of the classroom, where they were forgotten about until they were returned to us on the last day of school nine months later.

Charlie grunts, and I can hear the shuffle of something—his arm or leg—as he tries to move. He sucks in a breath. Hisses through his teeth.

The pain in my arm has a heartbeat. Does Charlie's? I pat the ground around me. Hard and gritty. I remember the stains on this floor and the way it looked like it hadn't been washed in years. The wads of gum stuck along the edges of the tables. I'm lying on top of this and underneath that now. I'm living and breathing in filth. All of it seeping into me.

I need a distraction.

I need to think about something to keep me from focusing on the *thump, thump, thump* of my body.

I think of the safest place. Home. With its warm blankets and hot showers. My mom in the kitchen and the TV buzzing. And then I see Coach Sanchez there and my stomach knots.

"Are you from here?" I ask Charlie.

"Here-*ish*."

Wait. Was he my classmate? Should I know him? "Did you go to Pacific Shore?"

"Harbor."

"Ah, sure. Harbor. The charter school nobody wanted."

He laughs. "Yeah. Our motto was 'Better than public, too many losers for private.'" Another laugh. "I take it you went to Pacific."

"Not did. Still do."

"Oh. You're even younger than I thought." He coughs. "I didn't think kids from Pacific knew how to do their own laundry."

"Wow."

"Sorry. Just bitter. I wanted to go to Pacific."

"Why didn't you?"

"My parents said no." A grunt. "Their favorite word."

My mom says yes to everything because she wants me to live a life of experience. She says yes to things she probably shouldn't. But I'm glad she pushes me out of my comfort zone. "That sucks."

"They're parents. Ones who aren't thrilled I'm not at college right now. I've got a full scholarship. What a waste, right?"

"Wait. You finally got out of here and you decided to come back? Why?"

"Had to."

"What do you mean you had to?"

"There was some . . . stuff that happened. I'd rather not get into it." He coughs. "But my parents were so pissed, they wouldn't let me come home, so I've been crashing on my brother's couch. You'd think they'd give him a hard time for not having some illustrious career by now, but I guess since he works at the Apple Store in the Pacific Pavilion mall they think he's an actual genius."

"So you dropped out of college to sleep on your brother's couch?"

He laughs. "I sound like a real loser when you put it like that."

"Are you?"

"Probably."

"When I get out of this town, I'm never coming back." Some coaches have already talked to me about playing for them in college. I can't wait to go. I don't want to be someone who never leaves this place, finishing high school only to scoop ice cream at the same shop they've worked at since they were fifteen.

"I get it."

"I didn't actually come to the laundromat to do laundry," I blurt.

"Because you can't, right? Ha! I knew Pacific Shore kids didn't know how to work those fancy buttons." He sounds so satisfied that it makes me smile.

"I guess I walked right into that one."

"You kind of did, Ruby's Diner." He laughs again. "So why did you come here if you're not a couch-surfing college dropout like me?"

"Truth?"

"Sure. Why the hell not?"

"The laundromat's where my friends and I find deadbeats to buy us beer."

"And I was your deadbeat?"

"You were a contender." I jiggle my right foot, trying to shake out the pins and needles that numb my toes.

"I may be a deadbeat, but I'm only nineteen. And even if I were twenty-one, I wouldn't have contributed to the corruption of a minor. Especially one who can't even do her own laundry."

"Why not?"

"Too much pressure. What if something happened to you after you drank the beer I bought you? I don't need that on my conscience."

"Okay, Dad." I snort. But then I think of Mila and how this should be a legit concern for anyone who buys her alcohol.

"Also? I don't drink."

"Ever?" I ask, surprised.

"Anymore."

"Why?"

"Reasons."

I try to shift my weight to ease up on where my shoulder is digging into the ground, but there isn't enough room. "Sounds like there's a story there."

"Not one I want to share."

"You were advocating for truth-telling five seconds ago. Who am I going to tell anyway?"

"It's not that. I just don't like thinking about it. Fine with me if I'm a hypocrite."

Silence.

"So do I get your college-dropout story instead?"

He sighs. "Maybe later. I'm tired." At first I think he means he's tired of this conversation, but then he yawns.

It's too early for him to be tired. I'm scared for him to fall asleep. I'm scared of the silence. I'm scared of being alone. I'm scared he won't wake up.

"Why are you tired? Is it because you're hurt?"

"Been up since six. For work. At the gym."

"You work at a gym?" I probably shouldn't conjure up his buff biceps, but I do. "I thought maybe you painted houses."

"What? Why?"

Is this the part where I tell him how I was watching his every move before the earthquake? "Because you had blue paint on your hands. And your chin. Before. When I saw you."

"Hm. Observant. I do paint. But not houses."

"That's cool. I'm not artistic."

"Not sure I am, either."

"So you don't paint houses but you do work at a gym."

"Yep. I quit Stanford to get a job at a gym. How's that for aiming high?"

"I'm not commenting on a story you haven't even told me. And by the way, I get up before six every day and I'm not tired."

"Are you a farmer?"

"No. I have workouts before school. For water polo."

"That's the sport where they swim up and down in Speedos with the ball, right?"

"It's slightly more complicated than that, but sure."

"We only had tennis at Harbor. Stanford has a water polo team, though. I've never seen an actual game, but some of those guys lived in my dorm." He laughs. "Cocky bastards. I guess that's what happens when you walk around ninety percent naked all day. But it's a real sport?"

"Are you kidding? It's one of the most demanding sports you

can possibly play. It's like basketball. *In the water.* You have to be in really good shape."

"Okay, but how hard can it be if you can touch the bottom of the pool?"

"You can't touch the bottom. The water's too deep. That's kind of the whole point."

"Sorry—you tread water and throw a ball around. Doesn't sound that rigorous."

"You aren't *treading* water. You have to move your legs like those attachments on an electric mixer. It's called eggbeater."

"And you think that's hard?"

I feel like I'm meeting one of my mom's new boyfriends all over again, and trying to explain what water polo is. I guess that's one advantage to her dating Coach Sanchez.

"Treading water isn't hard," Charlie says.

"It's not treading water." I clench my fists. "When you tread water it's because you're tired, right? You need to rest and catch your breath. You don't eggbeater to rest. It takes a lot of energy, and you do it to stabilize your body so you can throw the ball and wrestle people off you. Try scoring a goal while getting pulled, beaten, and dunked. Try throwing passes and stealing balls without ever resting. Try that for an hour and see what you think."

"Okay, okay. You've convinced me."

"Stanford has one of the best programs in the nation, by the way."

"There are a lot of 'one of the best programs in the nation' at Stanford. Ask my parents. They wanted me to major in all of them."

"Ha."

"So tell me this: If water polo is so hard, why would you want to do it on purpose?"

"Because I can."

MILA

Mila thought she could do anything.

Even when she was drunk.

Especially when she was drunk.

And ever since her mom and dad's divorce, Mila was drunk more than she should have been.

On New Year's Eve, she decided we all needed beer because there was a party and moonlight and a night full of possibilities. She knew how to get it as soon as she spotted a guy all sideways-leaning against the wall of the laundromat. The guy wore jeans and a tight black shirt with an unzipped jacket, and he had a buzz cut clipped so close you couldn't even tell what color his hair was.

"Ding ding ding," Mila said, like we'd won the grand prize on a game show.

"That guy?" I said. "He's so—"

"Gullible?"

I rolled my eyes. "That's mean."

Mila ran her tongue over her lip-glossed lips, looking like her sister, Lily, who'd finished high school before we'd gotten there. Lily was the one who usually provided Mila with an endless supply of alcohol, but I guess she was unavailable for once.

"Oh, Ruby. We'll probably make this guy's night," Mila said.

"I don't want to make this guy's night," Juliette said. "He looks old."

"Old*er*," Mila corrected her. "Not *old*."

"Fine," Thea said. "What's the plan?"

"Leo just gives them five dollars to do it," I pointed out. "Like a tip."

Mila rolled her eyes. "That's how it works if you're a guy."

"So what do we do?" Thea asked.

"Take your hair down," Mila told her. "Juliette, smile. Iris, hike up your skirt like mine."

"Ew," Iris said. "No."

Mila ignored her and looked at me. "You be your tall, gorgeous self with your ridiculous legs."

I instantly slumped. "Tall?"

"Um, hello. I also said gorgeous."

"And ridiculous," Thea said.

"Oh, please. Just be you. You're fine." Mila raked her fingers through her hair in a quick comb-through that left it looking all wavy like a mermaid's.

Mila led. We walked behind her like a row of ducklings following Mama Duck into oncoming traffic. The guy kept leaning as we got closer to the liquor store, but his eyes tracked us, watching where we went and how we moved. Once we were standing in front of him, he pushed off the wall and stood up straight.

"Girls," he said.

"Ladies," Mila said, reapplying her lip gloss.

He ran his hand across the top of his buzz cut, then smiled a big white row of teeth. "Need something?" he said.

Thea, Iris, Juliette, and I huddled together behind Mila, like we were doing one of those silly team-building drills Coach made us do last year where we had to gather behind a teammate and catch them when they fell.

"We were wondering," Mila said, "if you could do us a little favor."

"Oh, yeah?"

"Yeah." She smiled. "Do you think maybe you could buy us some beer?"

He grinned that grin again. It made him look knowing and dangerous all at once. "How old are you?"

I figured that was it. No way was he going to get tangled up buying beer for a bunch of high schoolers.

"Twenty," Mila said with so much confidence even I almost believed it.

"Really?" He smirked. "You sure about that?"

"I swear. Just a few months shy of my birthday. But we're stuck here killing time before heading back to college." She pouted, then inspected her fingernails. "Can't get out of this town fast enough, you know what I mean?" She leaned in conspiratorially. "So what do you think? Can you help us?"

"Depends. Do I get to share this beer with you?"

My brain was screaming, *Abort, abort!* but Mila kept going.

"Sure." She turned to us. "That's not a problem, right?"

Thea's mouth popped open, but she shut it again when Mila raised her eyebrows in a warning glare that said, *Don't even.*

At least there were five of us and only one of him.

"Sounds fun," Juliette said.

"Seriously?" Iris muttered under her breath. "Helping my grandma use the bathroom sounds more fun."

"See?" Mila said to the guy. "It's perfect."

"Okay then." He crossed his arms over his chest, which made him instantly look a million times bigger and stronger. Like a bouncer outside those skeevy dive bars by the pier where the drunks hung out to day drink. "I assume you're paying?"

Mila dug into the front pocket of her skirt and pulled out a ten. "Whatever you can get with this."

He laughed. "So not the good stuff?"

"Just do your best," Mila said. "Feel free to pitch in for something better if you want. We'll meet you over there at that parking lot behind the bank."

She pointed across the street and his gaze followed. My own gaze snagged on Sundial Circle—the stretch of sidewalk in the middle of town where all the skaters hung out. I scanned the crowd for Leo but only spotted a girl I knew from my astrophysics class as she went flying off a concrete bus bench on her board with her arm stretched out behind her. All I could think was how much more I wanted to be skateboarding over there than talking to this guy over here.

"You girls are a trip," the guy said, shoving the ten into his back pocket. "I'll meet you in five."

CHAPTER FIVE

6:42 P.M.

I TRY CALLING MY MOM AGAIN BUT STILL can't get a connection. I think of our last conversation. About Coach Sanchez. And the romantic getaway. And me losing my shit. *You've ruined my life.* Some of the last words I said to her.

And why? Because she fell in love? Because she found someone she actually wants to be with after I leave for college? Is that really the worst thing that ever could've happened to me? Because it could very well be the best thing that ever happened to her. After my dad died when I was four months old, my mom sank all her energy into a doctorate degree and work. But now she could have love, too, and I don't want her to. All because I'm afraid of how it will make *me* look.

I've got only thirty-seven percent left on my phone's charge, but I allow myself one more glance at my lock screen. It's a photo

Leo took of us in front of my locker before the first-period bell rang on the first day of school. He told me to smile at the camera, but then he surprised me with a kiss on my cheek at the last minute. The picture is slightly blurry and a little bit sideways, but it captures me laughing and happy and whole, so the sight of it makes my heart hurt.

I dial Leo at the risk of losing another percentage point on my battery, but nothing happens, so I let the screen go dark and picture him in my head instead. I see him with his skateboard dangling from his fingertips and his backpack slung over his shoulder, waiting for me outside the gate of the pool deck. Telling me about his own afternoon workout or his homework load for the night. Leaning over and kissing me even though I smell like chlorine and sunblock. I want to be there with him now. But instead I'm sweaty and cold all at once, with sticky armpits and a bloody sweatshirt and chattering teeth. I smell like this laundromat. Like dirt and wood rot and the dank mildew scent of leftover washing machine water. I'm sure that smell has crept into every square inch of my skin and hair follicles. Festering.

The blood on my sweatshirt is dry now. The sleeve is hard and crackly and pulling at the fine hairs on my arm as the winter darkness of a February evening takes over. There isn't light coming from that sliver above me anymore. A little less hope.

I try to stretch my back. I twist one way and then the other. My muscles are cramping, and I want to be able to stand up and extend my arms high over my head to stretch the way I do before a game. But nothing in here is the way it is out there.

This space is too quiet.

Charlie is too quiet.

I whisper his name through the dark.

He doesn't answer, and I call out louder.

More silence.

What if?

No. I can't think it.

"Charlie!" I yell. "Answer me!"

"Shit," he hisses. "What is it? I'm here."

The sound of his voice is a relief. Hope again.

"Don't do that. Don't make me think I'm here alone."

"Don't worry. It was just a catnap."

A catnap. That's what my mom used to tell me when I was four and started protesting weekend naps because I'd gotten old enough to know what I'd be missing while I was asleep. Sprinklers and swings and snacks and shows. Time with her after a long week of work and school. My mom would settle me in her own bed, surrounded by her pillows and her safe mom scent. She'd smooth my hair back from my face.

"It's just a catnap," she'd say.

"Meow," I'd say back, and she'd smile.

"Sleepy kitten. Close your eyes. Think of balls of yarn as blue as the sky. And walking through the tall green grass. And bowls of cold milk."

"Meow," I'd say again, softer this time. I was seeing all she wanted me to imagine and I'd push my hand across my face, pretending it was a paw. "Meow."

My mom would keep petting my head, a relaxing, perfect rhythm that made my eyelids heavy.

"Sleep, little kitten," she'd say. "There will be plenty of time to play and see the big wide world when you wake up again."

"Hey, Ruby?" There's an uptick in Charlie's voice that interrupts my kitten dreams. I can tell he has a new thought. A new worry.

"Yeah?"

"Should we be concerned about a gas leak or carbon monoxide poisoning? Asking for a friend."

I hadn't even thought of those things. What does carbon monoxide poisoning feel like? Would we drift off to sleep and not know we were dying?

"Ruby? Did you hear me?"

"I'm thinking." Wouldn't we already be dead if there was a carbon monoxide leak? "Isn't that what those switches were on that panel? The ones the lady turned off?"

It's a flash of a memory. That woman's final act of heroism. Trying to save a laundromat from going up in flames. Trying to save Charlie and me from whatever could've happened if those switches had stayed on. How did she have the good sense to do that but then run out into the parking lot where she could've been killed by flying debris? Electrocuted by a downed power line. She probably didn't survive. Sometimes people know one thing but not another when it comes to earthquake safety. There are people who think you're still supposed to huddle in a doorframe, but I learned from drills at school that they changed that a few years ago. Maybe she was trying to get to the doorway but decided outside looked like a better option.

"I thought that was an electrical panel," Charlie says.

"I think it was an emergency shutoff system for everything. Don't you have to have those in California? We have one at our house. You barely have to jostle it and it turns off. I hit it once when I was moving the trash cans to the curb, and my mom lost hot water in the middle of her shower."

"So you think we're okay?"

I feel the pressure of having to say the right thing because when Charlie isn't calm, I'm not calm. And we have to stay calm. I need him to stay calm for me.

"I'm sure. That lady saved us, Charlie."

"I wish we could thank her." I hear that tiny tick of worry finally slipping like fingers loosening their grip on the wet rungs of a ladder.

"Yeah," I say, even though my words aren't entirely true.

Because that woman might've saved us from gas leaks and carbon monoxide poisoning, but she didn't really *save* us.

We're still here.

CALM

I met Leo outside the gate of the pool after practice yesterday. He held my hand as we took a shortcut through the back parking lot. I wanted to keep our fingers twisted together forever. We walked two blocks to his car on the hill by the house with the mailbox that looks like a lifeguard tower. Red rescue can and all.

We drove the streets home without talking. We didn't need to.

We stood in my kitchen, where I made toast and swept up the crumbs with my hand. Leo ate four pieces with peanut butter while I went for cinnamon sugar.

He was standing there the way he always was. Looking the way I liked. Comfortable. Assured. Beautiful.

So I led him to my room.

Where it was only us.

Only then.

We ignored the knock on the front door from the UPS driver.

We ignored the minutes passing.

And the weather.

And the airplanes overhead.

The only thing we paid attention to was the moment. And the music on low. And the violet scarf over the lampshade that made my room look like twilight while our skin melded and our breath hitched.

CHAPTER SIX

8:00 P.M.

MY RIGHT CALF MUSCLE CRAMPS. LIKE IT'S
being held tight in someone's fist. Clenching. Clawing. Pulling. I
point my toes up. Stretch. It's not deep enough. It won't untwist.
I grunt through the spasm.

Charlie hears me. Asks what's wrong.

"Leg cramp."

"Oh, yeah. I've got those, too."

"Why didn't you say anything?"

"Didn't want to complain."

"I'm not complaining."

"You're definitely in the ballpark of complaining."

"Nope. I'm okay. I've handled worse pain in water polo."

Why am I so proud of this? Why do I need him to know?
Why do I want to explain that my sport is pain? That I know the

slice of someone else's fingernails digging into my skin as I fight for position in front of the goal. I know twisted nipples and thighs left purple and bruised. I know kicks to tender spots and private parts. I know scratches so deep they need Neosporin. I know muscles longing for ibuprofen and a body that feels like it can't walk another step without collapsing.

Maybe I need to remind myself because playing water polo makes me feel all the things I don't feel right now. Strong. Confident. Powerful.

When you're on a swim team, you eventually see water polo. The first time I saw it, I was ten years old.

I wanted to be like them.

It was so much more exciting than swimming back and forth by myself, from one end of the pool to the other, following a single black line and the thoughts in my head.

"I want to do that," I told my mom as she shoved my goggles and swim cap into the bag over her shoulder.

I went to my first practice two weeks later. I loved it from the second my hand touched the ball. I'd found exactly where I belonged in the water.

"I'm okay with the pain here," I say to Charlie. "But I could do without the fear."

"And the hunger."

"Yes. My stomach feels so empty." Hunger has crept in on tiptoes, punching at the hollow space of my belly. Grumbling. Growling. "I want a cold fruit and yogurt smoothie. Extra ice." I want it to slide down my dry throat, coating and cooling until it settles in my stomach and fills the emptiness inside me. "The last thing I ate was a bagel at breakfast." Breakfast. Where Mila was obnoxious. That already seems so long ago.

"I had a banana. We definitely could've done better."

My hollow belly rumbles. "Well, my stomach just growled over a banana, so . . ."

Charlie laughs. "Yeah. Same here. Not to mention your smoothie with all the ice."

I think of eating dinner with my mom. I think of her wavy hair and her eye crinkles and her belly laugh and her recipes and her no-phones-at-the-table rule. I think of backyard meals in the summer and bowls of soup on the couch in the winter.

I think of dinner last night and yelling and pushing my chair back and stomping off. If I could go back there now, I would. I would stay at the table for the rest of my life if it meant I could talk to her. I would explain why I was upset. That her dating my coach hurt me, and made me feel left out in my own life. But then I would listen to her, too.

If I had known what today would be, I would've let her in my room last night. I would've felt the way my bed shifted when she sat down. I want to be in my room again. With my mom. Where our problems are so much smaller than these ones.

Because it seems too easy to be left here.

With the fear of never seeing her again.

Never being able to tell her I'm sorry.

And that knowledge is the worst pain of all.

MOM AND DAD

My mom likes to tell me the story of the day she met my dad. It was in a beach town in Italy in the summer after her last year of college. She says she tells me the story so I'll remember him somehow, even if it's my mom who needs to remember.

Sometimes I feel bad that I don't hurt the way she does. But how am I supposed to mourn the loss of someone I never knew?

"He had earrings and this mass of Kurt Cobain hair. He looked like he should be in a band. He was cool. Cooler than me."

My mom's thinking long hair and earrings were cool always makes me smile.

When she talks, I can hear the drift in her voice as the memories seep in. She is twenty-two. She is seeing the world with a backpack and a best friend. She is suddenly in that beach town, with that sea breeze and her sunburn, and she's seeing my dad for the first time, as the salty wind whips his hair around.

Okay, maybe they were kind of cool.

"He thought I was someone he knew," she says, and smiles. "And when I wasn't, he said, 'Well, then, you're someone I would like to know.'"

So cheesy. But I could never make fun of her love story.

She tells me often about the way he surfed. And the way he told jokes. And the way he laughed. And the way he lived.

"He really, really *lived*," she always says then sighs. And maybe that makes it better somehow. That he crammed more into thirty years than most people cram into a lifetime.

There were Santa Anas on the day my dad died. Hot, dry winds that made the coast feel like the desert. There's a history behind them. A lore. People think they're ominous, ushering in change and madness, unsettling the balance of things, uprooting trees and rustling your hair like ghostly fingers scratching at the nape of your neck. My mom always spoke of them with such reverence that, when I was younger, I thought they had been a critical piece of my dad's story. As if they'd officially played a role. As if they'd had the literal power to scoop up my dad and turn him into wildfire ash at the charred foothills of Southern California.

My mom pushes her wavy hair behind her shoulders when she tells me memories, twists a curly strand around one finger. Drops it. Twists another. Lost in thought. She has the same wavy hair as me, minus the damage from years of pool water and sunshine.

My mom smells like summer. Like gardenia flowers and lemonade.

She talks back to Siri like they're having an actual conversation. She even tells her thank you when she's done taking directions.

She sneaks zucchini layers into her lasagna and I pretend not to notice.

She loves fireplaces and poems and beach days in no particular order.

She thinks she takes good photos but half the time someone's head is cut off or the frame is crooked or the light is bad.

I got my hair and my love of sunsets and beaches and bad reality TV from her.

My mom says I got my height and my love of the water from my dad.

My parents spent three weeks together in Italy after they met. When my dad went to Greece, they thought it would end. But it didn't.

"That's what love is," my mom says when she talks about it. "Never-ending."

My mom's original intent that summer she met my dad was to come home in August and start her dream job of working to save the oceans. Instead she said goodbye to her friends at a train station in London, then spent the next year passing through quaint villages and seashore towns with my dad. And when that year of travel ended, they came back to California and got married a few months later on an autumn evening at city hall right before closing time.

Five years later, she got pregnant with me.

But on a Monday morning four months after I was born, my dad was walking in the middle of a crosswalk with a cup of coffee in his hand and was hit by a distracted driver. He spent four days in the hospital on life support, waiting for his mom and dad and brother and sister to have a chance to say goodbye. And then my mom signed the papers to let him go.

I hate hospitals. Hospitals are where people go to die.

My dad's family went home after the funeral and then it was just my mom and me.

And my mom became weighed down by the memories of what was and the dreams that would never be.

But last night at dinner, my mom said Coach Sanchez was special. The look on her face told me it was *real*. It's taken her so long to get here. It's not about me. But last night I made it that way.

CHAPTER SEVEN

9:19 P.M.

THE EARTH BUCKS UNDERNEATH ME. I THINK
it's a bad dream at first. I want it to be a bad dream.

But then I remember.

It's happening again. An aftershock. Why is it happening again? I clamp down on my fear. I knot my hands and squeeze my eyes shut.

"Goddammit!" Charlie shouts.

I tell myself this is normal. That after earthquakes there are aftershocks. Smaller swells as the earth settles into its new space. The ground sways. Things that didn't crash to the ground the first time crash to the ground now. I can only hope the teetering table and the fragile walls around us won't break down completely. If they do, we'll be crushed. We can't get lucky twice. We might not even be lucky once.

I am a pill bug in the middle of my kindergarten rug.

Scrunched. Clenched. Unsure.

I can't see what's happening through the dark.

This jolt is big enough but it's nowhere near the original magnitude 7.8. It rains more dust. More dirt. It lands like hard sprinkles on my face. It reminds me of the strangest thing. It reminds me of my mom grating fresh Parmesan cheese over my spaghetti noodles when I was five.

"Say when," she'd say, but I'd never say it. "When?" she'd finally ask me again, and I'd nod.

I am spaghetti noodles. I am limp arms and lifeless legs. I am mush.

The rumbling ground smacks against my helpless body.

Until it stops.

Charlie and I lie still in the silence, bracing ourselves for the earth to move again. Holding our breath. Waiting to speak.

"Well, that sucked," Charlie finally says.

"Are you okay?"

"Think so." He coughs. "That was one hell of an aftershock."

My brain can't hide my fear. *What if something bigger hits?* That's what happened in Ridgecrest in July 2019. On the morning of the Fourth of July, there was an earthquake, a magnitude 6.4, and it was big enough for some people to feel it up and down the coast even though the damage was minimal. But the next day, there was a bigger one. A magnitude 7.1. And experts talked about foreshocks and how what you feel the first time might only be a hint of what's to come. Can this laundromat survive something bigger? Can we? I try to picture the earth settling in a more peaceful way. Of cracks and crevices spooning each other, then falling asleep. Anything to calm me down. But it doesn't help. "I'm kind of freaking out, Charlie."

"Don't freak out." He shuffles in his space. "Can you just close your eyes?"

"Done."

"I guess I'll have to trust you."

"Duh."

"Think of someplace big. Somewhere with wide-open space." I feel the peace in his voice, the calm he's extending to me. I bet his eyes are closed, too, trying to go to that wide-open space with me. "Feel it. Smell it. Like you're there. Like you're home."

I suck in a breath, trying to transport myself. Trying to imagine.

"Where are you?"

"The beach. Hawaii." The sun's heating my toes and fingertips. I see Mila on a towel next to me, the fuzzy buzz of a pop song seeping out from her AirPods, interrupting my calm. I want to yank her AirPods out and make her go away.

"What's the water like?"

"Turquoise blue. Clear." I'm glad Charlie's question makes me focus on something else. On the waves lapping the wet brown-sugar sand.

"Do you spend a lot of time in Hawaii? Is that a required school trip for kids who can't do their own laundry?"

"Hardly. But I've gone the past three summers. For water polo tournaments."

I tell Charlie that last summer Mila convinced us to sneak out past bed check to hang out with a boys' team at the hotel pool because they had tequila and a hot team captain. Mila got drunk in record time, then insisted I balance her on my shoulders so she'd have a height advantage as she wrestled a guy from the other team in a water jousting match. I can still feel the way my fingers dug into the soft skin above her knees as I tried to steady her. I was concerned she'd get hurt even though it was my neck feeling like it might break as it twisted with her body. I worried about how mad Coach would be if I injured myself and couldn't play the next day, so after Mila won, I swam away and stood in the shallow end with Iris, letting the warmth of the underwater lights heat my legs. *Why are we here?* I'd asked Iris. *There's nothing in this for us except getting in trouble.* She'd shrugged. We were there because someone had to look out for Mila.

"Rebels. Did you get caught for sneaking out?" Charlie says.

"Not all of us. Only Mila. I thought she'd gone to bed but I guess she'd snuck out again. Security called our room at two a.m., told us to come get our friend." I'd shoved my feet into flip-flops and run down in my pajamas to get her. She'd thrown up and broken the glass tequila bottle on the pool deck. I was so afraid Coach would find out and she'd get sent home. The next day she had a hangover so we told Coach it was food poisoning. He didn't buy it. But he didn't have proof we were lying. "Karma was that she lost her championship ring in the pool. Probably down the drain. She was more upset about that than anything."

"Seems like Mila's got bigger problems than lost jewelry."

She does. But I can't go there. "The ring was special. We all got one for winning our division in water polo last year. I'm wearing mine now." I spin it around my finger. "I don't always wear it."

"So why today?"

"Because I'm thinking about quitting water polo."

"Um, Ruby? Have you met you? You're basically in love with water polo. You'd marry it if you could. And have little Speedo babies."

"Yeah. But my mom started dating my coach."

"That's awkward."

"Right? And the team thinks I'm getting special treatment."

"Are you?"

"I don't think so."

"Then I'm not really seeing a reason for quitting something you love."

"Didn't you love school?"

"Yeah."

"But you still quit."

"Right."

"Why? What's your big reason that's so much better than mine?"

"Something happened."

"*Something*'s pretty vague."

He sighs. "I know."

"Tell me what happened, Charlie."

"I saw something. And when I saw it, I didn't do anything about it."

"What kind of something?"

"A death kind of something."

"Are you messing with me?"

"No. I wouldn't do that."

"Tell me."

"The thing is, if I tell you, then I have to hear it again. And you won't be able to unhear it. And I'm not sure that's good for either of us."

"I can handle it."

"I don't know if I can."

"Who died, Charlie?"

"Jason Cooper."

"Please tell me what happened."

"Why?"

"Because I think, deep down, you want to. I think Jason Cooper is the reason you're sleeping on your brother's couch and working out at the gym like you're training for the Olympics. I'd do the same thing if I were trying to forget bad memories."

"You seem to understand a lot about a lot, Ruby in the Rubble."

"I know about not doing something when maybe I should do something." I think of Mila. And her drinking. And the way I always wonder if I should speak up. Or out.

He's silent for a moment. "What do you know about fraternities?"

"Just TV and movie stuff."

"You know you have to rush, right? To join?"

"Yeah."

"Well, I thought I'd try it. Like maybe it'd be a way to meet some people. New place. New me. But, Ruby? That fraternity thing? It wasn't great. Too much alcohol. Too many dares. A lot of bad choices. And this guy, Jason, was embracing all three. Shot after shot after shot. It was like getting into that frat was the only thing that mattered. I should've noticed how bad off he was sooner. I should've said something. But freshmen don't get to speak up."

I think of all the times I wanted to say something. To talk to Mila about her drinking. And then every cautionary tale kids have ever been told encourages us to seek out a trusted adult—a counselor or a parent. Or a coach. But there's that word. *Trusted.* On what planet are teenagers instantly supposed to trust adults? I trusted my mom and Coach and they fell in love behind my back. Why should I trust anyone? I never said anything about Mila to any adult I knew because if none of the adults were noticing she had a problem, then maybe I was making too much of it anyway. Maybe she was fine.

"Death should be more complicated," Charlie says. "All Jason got was blackout drunk and a defibrillator that came too late. But if I'd done something sooner, maybe he'd only have a story about a too-drunk night at a fraternity party. It still would've been scary. He still would've had an ambulance ride and his stomach pumped, but he'd be alive."

"Jason dying isn't your fault, Charlie."

"It *feels* like it's my fault."

"Did you stay with him? When he was like that?"

"I put him on his side. Some other guys propped him up with

his backpack. That's the big college trick. All the kids are doing it, don't you know?" He rustles in his rubble. "Guess what? It doesn't work."

I've seen Mila passed out so many times. It's scary. And I'm always afraid she might not wake up. "But you didn't leave him, Charlie."

"I stayed with him until the ambulance came. But he was already gone when they got there."

"That's what matters. That you were with him until the end."

"It didn't matter. He died."

"It mattered, Charlie. Being with someone in their last minutes matters."

He's quiet. Thinking.

"Are you okay?" I ask.

"I keep trying to make sense of it. I thought if I took a semester off, I'd figure it out. That I'd want to go back. But I don't. I hate Stanford. And I used to love it. It was my water polo, Ruby. Not that it matters now. I mean, definitely not now. Look at us—trapped here." He groans. "The best part is my parents think I quit because I couldn't handle Stanford. And I couldn't. But not for the reasons they thought. I couldn't handle *life*. There's going to be a court case. Jason's parents want answers. Our fraternity was suspended. There were news crews around all the time. I just had to . . . leave."

"I get it."

"And pretty soon I'll have to sit in some courtroom and tell everyone how I let a kid die."

"You didn't let anyone die, Charlie."

"You can say that a million times and I'll never believe you." He coughs. It's ragged and tired. "But this is all to say that I think it's important you keep your ring and your game and your team. You still won the championship last year. You earned that ring. Be proud of it. Don't let the stuff you love slip away." He coughs again. "Listen to me, I'm like a public service announcement for how to not be a couch-surfing college dropout."

"You need to stop talking about yourself like that."

"Like what?"

"Like you're some loser. Because you're not." I clear my throat. Cough out the dust. "I'll make you a deal. I'll give *you* my ring. You hold on to it until you're ready to love Stanford again. Because I think, with a little time, you'll love the stuff you loved again. We both will. And when that happens, I'll take my ring back."

"I like that. Holding on to your ring."

"Okay. It's done. That's the plan."

"I should give you something, too."

"Great. You pick."

He hums as he thinks. "How about my journal? That's the thing I'd be most devastated to lose."

I feel bad for almost rolling my eyes when I first saw Charlie and his journal. He didn't deserve that. "I'll protect it at all costs. And I won't even crack it open if you don't want me to."

"It's okay. You can read it and tell me if I'm any good."

"Deal."

"I'd shake hands on it but, you know. Rubble."

"Your promise is good enough for me."

The laundromat is dark. The sirens are echoes. The minutes are swirling. Charlie is quiet, lost in his guilt and his memories.

"What happened wasn't your fault, Charlie." I say it again because I believe it. And I want him to believe it, too.

PROMISES

When I turned up to my first day of club water polo at ten years old, I expected to find a team of girls like I'd met when I played soccer. It turned out the ten-and-under team was mixed, meaning boys and girls played on teams together. Besides me, there was only one other girl on my team: Mila.

Even at ten years old, the boys had already created a bro-club culture, and Mila and I were the odd girls out. When we went to tournaments, the boys traveled in a pack, while Mila and I hung together on the outskirts. No matter. We fought our way to earn starting positions. She played goalie. I played the field.

One day, as we warmed up before a game, the boys took shot after shot at the goal. Mila consistently blocked each attempt, proving every ounce of her All-America status.

"Watch Ruby," Tanner said when it came my turn to shoot. "Bet she throws like a girl."

"Duh. I am a girl." I raised my arm, gripped the ball, and aimed at the right corner of the goal. My shot flew past Mila's outstretched fingertips and into the net—the first goal of the day.

Mila glared at Tanner and yelled, "Yeah, Ruby throws like a girl all right. Too bad you don't."

Later, when we were sitting on the pool deck, drinking water and sharing a granola bar after the game, I asked Mila if she'd missed my shot on purpose.

She looked at me, her eyes nearly shiny with hurt. "Why would I do that?"

"Because the boys were being jerks. As usual."

"They were, but you made the goal. I missed it. I promise."

"Okay, good."

"We're the only girls here," she said, handing me another bite of the granola bar. "We have to stick together."

"I know."

"We should come up with a secret handshake or something." She tapped her fingertip to her chin, thinking. "How about something like this?" I followed along as she pinkie-promised our pinkies, made jazz hands, high-fived, led us into a legit handshake, and ended by pulling our hands apart and doing some weird thing of rubbing her fingertips together. "I'm sprinkling glitter," she said as she danced her dangling fingers above the ground. "Because we can like glitter and kick butt at the same time."

"I love glitter," I said. "I wish I could put it on everything."

"They should make glitter water polo balls."

We agreed that that would be the best.

We also agreed we would be the best at water polo and the best at being friends.

Too bad it didn't last.

CHAPTER EIGHT

11:00 P.M.

MY EYELIDS DROOP. HEAVY. LIKE WEIGHTS are pulling them down. I take a quick peek at my phone. Eleven o'clock at night. I attempt to dial my mom but get nothing. Again. Six hours of nothing.

On school nights, I'm usually finishing up homework and going to bed right now. On a typical Friday night, eleven o'clock would be my curfew. I'd just be getting home, putting on my pajamas, logging into Netflix, and firing off one last text to Leo. I'd crawl between the cool sheets of my bed and tuck the puffy purple comforter underneath my chin.

I want to be there.

I want to hear the sounds of my house falling asleep.

I want to hear the hum of late-night television through the

wall to my mom's room. Her faint laugh over a joke from the opening monologue.

I want the soft flicker of the night-light in the hallway.

I want to sink into my mattress.

I want to drift.

I want to dream.

But I'm stuck on this hard slice of cold ground in a darkness so dark it fills me with fear. My thoughts narrow to focus on different points of pain. My head. My arm. My right elbow screams loudest, the knot of it bruised from grinding into the ground like the mortar and pestle set my mom uses to smash garlic cloves. The skin is rubbed raw. The simple thought of the Minnie Mouse Band-Aids my mom used to put on my cuts when I was a kid makes me want to cry.

Charlie mumbles in the dark. His words a chant under his breath. The sound has kept me company for the last hour, the repetition somehow soothing. His words aren't loud enough for me to decipher, so I let him keep his secrets. Maybe he's processing what he told me. I want to tell him over and over again that what happened isn't his fault. But I understand the way he needs to be quiet with himself right now.

There's a slow build to a new spot of pain. Like it's growing. Expanding. Pushing.

My bladder.

I have to pee. I have to pee so bad that my insides ache.

I can't hold it any longer.

I close my eyes like it will somehow hide what I'm doing.

I'm about to pee my pants.

On purpose.

I want to make noise with my hands to drown out the sound of it, so I pat them against the sides of my legs.

And then I relax enough to go.

The relief is instant and makes me sigh. The way I've felt on long road trips after scanning the horizon for an exit and finally finding a bathroom. My pee is warm at first, almost hot against my body that's gone so cold, I'd be lying if I said it doesn't feel good. Is it gross to think my pee feels like a warm bath? Yes. But then there's the smell of urine mixing with the ground grime and I want to gag.

Charlie rustles.

Can he smell it? Does he know?

Has he gone pee himself?

In between his mumbling he's been breathing tight, short, shallow breaths, which worry me. The labored sound of them. I tell myself he's okay because I have to believe he is.

Because I don't know what else I'm supposed to do.

Last fall, our school participated in the Great ShakeOut Earthquake Drill. It was supposed to teach all of us how to survive earthquakes. The drama department coordinated the whole thing like it was the spring musical instead of preparation for the worst thing that might ever happen to us. Mila played someone with a broken leg. There were triage tents on the football field—one for the dead and one for the dying. Coach tagged bodies in the dead tent.

Leo and I watched from the bleachers while sucking on Tootsie Pops. It was an excuse to get out of class early. I should've paid closer attention. I should've taken notes.

I miss Leo. I want him here now.

A thought creeps in. One I've kept squashing.

What if he isn't okay?

Would I sense it? If he's gone? Leo with his chlorine curls and his crooked smile, with one AirPod plugged into his head. In his flip-flops and his board shorts and his sweatshirt with the broken zipper. Leo who does a perfect imitation of our AP English teacher reading Shakespeare sonnets out loud. Leo who rides a skateboard to school and carries an endless supply of Cuties oranges. Leo who presses his fingers into the small of my back in the hallway between classes, making me want to grab his face and kiss him all the way through sixth period. Leo who understands me.

He has to be okay.

He wouldn't have been on campus yesterday evening.

He would've been at home.

With his little brother.

Who he would've done everything to protect.

There are people who walk away from earthquakes. Even The Big One. People without badges and hard hats rush into toppled buildings to help. I know this. I've seen it. On television. Ordinary people doing extraordinary things.

That is what Leo would do. That is where he'd be. I'm sure of it.

But who was on campus and who wasn't when the earthquake hit? There would've been sports teams and band practice and after-school activities. There would've been soccer teams on the football field and basketball players in the gym.

I can see it. The buildings of Pacific Shore broken apart like this laundromat.

And all of the people I know who might've been inside them.

I think of the girl in my US government class who kicks ass on Model UN. Is she okay, or was she flattened in a car underneath a broken freeway overpass? And the boy who built the robot that won a national contest and a five-hundred-dollar prize. Is he okay, or is he trapped inside the lab at school where the robotics club works on projects deep into the night? What about the college-and-career-center counselor who helped me compose an email to the coach at Cal? Is she okay, or did she get crushed like Charlie?

The water polo team was in the pool. My friends. My teammates. Coach. What happened there? Did Coach tell everyone what to do like he always does? Was he right? Did they listen? Did he make things better or worse? Or could he not help? Because he isn't okay?

I wonder these things.

My own version of what happened.

But I don't know if it's true.

I don't know what is and isn't true anymore.

LIES

We huddled underneath the crackling glow of a fluorescent light in the bank parking lot, waiting for the guy with the buzz cut to bring Mila the beer she couldn't go a weekend without. While we were waiting, Thea took a selfie. Iris sifted through her Snaps. Juliette blew her bangs from her forehead. I envied the skaters at Sundial Circle. Mila de-hiked her skirt and eyed the front door of the liquor store, worrying her hands into knots over the idea that this guy might take off with her alcohol.

"Seriously. What's the plan now?" Thea asked. "Because there's no way I'm actually drinking with this dude."

"Maybe we have a couple with him," Mila said.

"But he's old," Juliette said.

Mila laughed. "We're practically eighteen. He can't be more than twenty-one. It's like three years. Like a freshman and a senior. Big deal."

"No, really. How are we bailing?" I said. Because I didn't want to hang out with this guy when I could be kissing Leo at midnight.

"Shh, here he comes." Mila stood straighter, smoothing and primping. "I promise I've got this. It's a drink, not a date."

"Are you sure about that? Because I'm not sure he is," I said.

We watched him cross the street. He was all swagger, cruising through the middle of Sundial Circle, where nobody looked at him. Nobody said hi. He was just a person who was there. But I wanted someone we knew to look. I wanted someone to notice. I wanted them to track him and see him walking toward us, so they'd come, too. Or at least remember.

"Girls," the guy said once he was standing right in front of us.

"Ladies," Mila corrected him again.

He ran his hand across his buzz cut. Smiled that big-toothed grin. "Right. Right."

I could hear the glass bottles clinking together in the paper sack under his arm when he moved. He didn't seem to be in a hurry to hand it over. Mila made a grab for it, but he pulled it out of her reach. She looked at me for help, but I wasn't about to wrestle him for beer I didn't even want. The whole thing had been a waste of time. I was sure there was plenty to drink at the party. Or someone had an older brother or sister home from college who could get something.

"So," he said.

"So." Mila eyed the bag. She was all flirty and batty eyelashes and more lip gloss and I was so fed up I could scream.

"So where are we going to drink this?" the guy said.

My friends and I looked at one another, wondering which one of us was going to tell him, *No thanks.*

"Oh, come on, I did you a favor. Now do me a favor and come hang out with me." He ran his free hand over his buzz cut.

Looked up at the moon in the sky. Sniffed. Looked back at us. Smiled. "This town is completely void of action. Entertain me."

Iris and Juliette took steps backward like they might make a run for it.

"Um—" Thea started, but Mila cut her off.

"Where do you want to go?" Mila said, blinking at him.

The guy looked around. Over his shoulder, across the drive-through ATM lane, and all the way to Sundial Circle as the wheels of a skateboard smacked down on the sidewalk with a splat. Then he looked the other way, past the old houses that had been transformed into quaint doctors' offices with their lights turned off for the night.

"Beach?" He switched the package from beneath one arm to the other. His shoulders got broader. His shirt got tighter. His jeans went looser.

"Meet you there?" Iris said.

He scrunched his eyebrows. "Why would you meet me there when we're already here together?"

"I need to get my car."

"I watched you walking from a block away."

Mila smiled. "Did you now?"

He smiled back. "You don't have a car here."

Mila took a step forward, her eyes on the beer. Because that's all she cared about. And if it took going with that guy to get it, she would go. If it meant taking us down with her, she would.

"My car is down the block," Iris said.

"So's the beach. Why would you walk down that block to go get your car when you can walk down this block and go to the beach?"

Mila took another step forward. Closer. Too close. "Excellent point," she said. "Lead the way."

DAY TWO

SATURDAY

CHAPTER NINE

1:13 A.M.

CHARLIE WAKES UP COUGHING THROUGH the dark. I check my phone. Note the time. It's been nine hours. I let in that tiny speck of light from the screen. No reception. No texts. No missed calls. Nothing. I should accept that my phone isn't going to save us.

"I'm so thirsty," Charlie says.

"Hungry." A mumble. Because I'm tired, too.

I haven't eaten since yesterday, and my stomach feels hollow like a carved-out jack-o'-lantern with all the juicy guts tossed aside. I picture the jack-o'-lanterns I carved as a kid and how, after days of baking in the sun, they'd keel over, caving in on themselves because their insides weren't full enough to stay upright. I imagine the hours passing in here and my belly rotting from the inside out in the same way. Until I fold over. Empty. Lifeless.

I want a pillowcase full of Halloween candy. Caramel apples. Buttered popcorn.

Halloween means big houses by the beach decorated like haunted pirate ships. With smoke machines and strobe lights and full-size candy bars. My mom would take me door-to-door in my Wonder Woman costume. Or later, in middle school, when my friends and I would come up with a group costume, our parents would let us go out alone. It felt like freedom to walk from one block to the next without our parents trailing behind us, waiting on the sidewalk with their flashlights while we knocked on doors.

Last Halloween, I took care of Mila at a Halloween party. It was in Harper Scott's backyard. There was a keg and a firepit and a hammock and a crowd. There was a koi pond, too. Mila dumped a can of beer into the water, giggling hysterically.

"Here, fishy fishy," she cooed, kicking up the water with her fingertip like it was a touch pool at the aquarium. "Wanna get drunk with me? Because Ruby won't."

"Stop! Do you want to kill them?"

She stomped her foot, and the spiked heel that went with her cat costume sank into the grass. She lost her balance. Toppled over. Landed on her knees. Spilled the rest of her beer. A crowd gathered because she wouldn't get up. Couldn't. She stayed there on all fours and laughed.

Until she was crying.

Everyone watched as she sank onto her back. Balled up into the fetal position.

"What's wrong?" I'd asked. Panicked.

She pulled me down next to her like she was going to tell me a secret. Like she was finally going to explain what it was she was always trying to numb. She put her hand on my cheek. Looked at me like I was the only one she could spill her truth to.

"What?" I said. "Tell me."

Her eyes glistened. Watery. Then she burst into laughter. "I can't feel my feet. Will you carry my shoes?"

"What?" I shook my head. I'd missed something. Surely.

"My shoes."

She kicked her feet up and down. I was afraid one of her spiked heels would go flying and take someone's eye out. So I yanked them off. Pulled her up. Made her put her arm around me as she stumbled to the car.

I'd wanted to put a wall up. A barrier that'd block our classmates from seeing her like this. But really? It was just another party. Just another weekend. And no matter how much I tried to protect Mila, everyone had seen her like this too many times to count.

I took her to her house that night. Tucked her into her bed and settled into a sleeping bag on the floor so I could keep an eye on her. I lied to her mom when she knocked on Mila's bedroom door. I told her she wasn't feeling well. It was the same excuse as always.

"A bunch of people got sick from this onion dip at the party," I'd said.

Mila's mom seemed like she'd believed me. So again, I questioned myself, wondering if I was overreacting. If Mila's own mom couldn't see a problem, then why should I be so concerned?

But maybe it was easier to pretend not to see things than to see the truth.

"My toes are freezing," I say to Charlie. "I need something better than flip-flops."

"Flip-flops in February. So typical." He coughs, then wheezes over his breath. He sucks in air. It doesn't sound good.

"Charlie!"

He coughs some more.

"Charlie!" I say again, that rise of panic in my throat.

He finally sputters to a stop. Like the earthquake.

"Yeah. Still here." He grunts. "I promise I'm not going anywhere unless you do."

CHAPTER TEN

2:00 A.M.

MY LEFT ARM IS HOT WHERE I CUT IT.
Throbbing. The heartbeat inside of it getting stronger.

Ba-thump, ba-thump, ba-thump.

The bleeding has long stopped, but that heartbeat and that hot, hot heat tell me it's angry.

"I think I need stitches, Charlie."

"On your arm?"

"Yeah."

We've been here way longer than I thought we would be. It's hard to hang on to hope when there's nobody else on the other side of this rubble. The dark and the cold have slithered in like a shadow. Taking over this space. Taking over me.

High above us helicopter blades swoop and swivel.

Womp, womp, womp.

They never stop. Each rotation is another second ticking away. *What's taking so long?*

Every time I try to move an arm or leg, it goes in slow motion. All of it stiff and wedged in place. What does it mean? To feel like I'm stuck in thick, sticky syrup? And that my arm is hot with a heartbeat?

"Can you have rigor mortis when you're still alive?" I ask.

"Try to move, even if only to wiggle your fingers or toes. Whatever you can do," he says. "You need to keep the blood flowing." He rustles in his space. "Force it." He talks like he knows something I don't. Something desperate. Something important.

"Why? What'll happen if I don't?"

"Just do it." He grunts. "If you do it, I'll feel like I know something. And since I don't know shit about most things, this'll make me feel less useless."

"You aren't useless."

I press down on the heat in my arm and feel the warmth seep into my fingertips. Too hot. "I'm a horrible person for saying this, but I'm so glad you're here, Charleston Smith."

"I get it, Ruby Tuesday. Your misery loves my company."

"It does."

"Are you moving? Are you keeping the blood flowing?" His breath is hitched with exertion.

I roll inches to my right then inches to my left. Back and forth. I knot my hands into fists and wiggle my toes. I jiggle my legs and arms as much as they'll give. I imagine the blood flowing through my veins. Feeding my cells. Pumping my heart.

"Tell me something," I say. "Distract me."

"You like questions?"

"Depends."

"Ones that are personal but not too personal?"

"My favorite kind." I smile, feeling the muscles move in my face, around my bones. Warming.

"What does college look like for you besides water polo? Like will you actually get a degree in something?"

"Ha ha."

"Now see? *Ha ha* isn't technically an answer. You've hinted at your plan to be a beast in the pool. Where do you want to go? You said Stanford has a good program."

"I want to go to Cal."

"Cal?" he sputters. "Are you saying that to mess with me? You do realize Stanford and Cal are hard-core rivals, right?"

"I'm aware."

Charlie responds with a tsk. "You're making this very hard on me, Ruby. I won't exactly be able to cheer you on at your water polo game when your school is *Cal.*"

I laugh. "Whatever."

"*Whatever?* Okay, fine. In the spirit of continuing to get along in our dire circumstances, let's dump the college rivalry . . . for now . . . What about books? Do you plan on cracking any? Picking a major?"

"Maybe biology. What was your major?"

"Art stuff. Creative writing. Film or theater. You know, all the things that pay the big bucks."

"Did you take those classes?"

"Not yet. Freshman year is all about knocking out require-ments. But I did try improv."

"That's a class?" I flutter my arms as far as they will go. Inches.

"It's a hobby. I was terrible, by the way. I'm not funny."

"But you are funny."

"Not according to my audition."

I move my legs. Inches up. Inches down. "Is improv really all about being funny? I thought it was about reacting to whatever gets thrown at you."

"Based on the fact that you already know that, you'd be better at improv than I was."

"Oh, come on. It can't have been that bad." I roll my neck.

"Oh, it was bad. Categorically. Abysmally."

I curl my toes. "What happened?"

"Are you sure you want to hear this?"

"Yes. *Please*. Tell me about how not funny you are."

He laughs. "Okay. Fine. So Stanford has this improv comedy troupe and when I went on my college tour, they were performing on the lawn in the middle of the day. I thought that was the coolest thing ever. To just be funny in the middle of the day at such a serious place. My parents had made it out like college would be four years of me putting my head down and working my ass off. Probably because of my scholarship and them being afraid I would screw it up. So to see anything that looked remotely fun was unexpected."

"And you joined immediately. Left the tour to run off with the improv circus?"

He snorts. "I had to audition. Once I got there. But I didn't make it, Rubik's Cube."

"Groan. That one was really bad, Charleston."

"Right. See? Not funny. You should have zero ounces of surprise that I didn't make it."

"What happened?"

"Well, everyone who wasn't me was really funny. So sharp. So quick." He snaps his fingers, and it's a relief to hear the sound of something so simple. "Their jokes legit made my hands sweat. But it's spontaneous, so I figured I'd come up with something good in the moment. I hadn't considered my nerves and my not being funny. Plus, I was in the last group to audition." He grunts. "It was a disaster."

"No, Charlie. *This* is a disaster. Bombing an audition is a party."

"Now see? That's a funny line, Ruby. Please keep improv in mind if you can find the time to do it in between all that eggbeater stuff you like to do."

"Okay, okay. So it was complete and utter humiliation for Charleston Smith. I want details."

I hear the scratch of his shuffles. "The scene was supposed to be about moving into your dorm and meeting your roommate and neighbors for the first time. Should've been easy enough given the fact that I'd literally just done that. Like two days before. But yeah. I basically froze. There were five of us in the scene. Two of them were pros. Seniors. They were the ones that kept changing the stuff around to help us newbies find our way to the jokes."

"Makes sense."

"So the scene turned into this bit about what was in the box I was carrying. The whole thing about improv is that you always have to say 'Yes, and' to whatever gets thrown at you. So then one of them says, 'Why is your box moving?' Suddenly, I had to act like the box was bouncing all over the place and I couldn't control it, like I had a living thing in there."

"I can picture it."

"But I knew someone was going to ask me what was in the box soon enough."

"So what was in it?"

"That's the thing. I had no idea. I didn't want to come up with something expected."

"Like a puppy?"

"Like a puppy." He coughs. "But I couldn't even focus on what was happening or what anybody else was saying because my brain just kept screaming, *What's in the box, dumbass?* I didn't really hear what anyone else was saying. It was like underwater echo sounds. So I never said what was in the box. I bombed. And when it was over, the seniors said thanks a lot and have a nice life."

"Brutal."

"Yeah." A chuckle. "It wasn't until I was walking back to my dorm that I realized *I* didn't need to be the one to come up with what was in the box. I just thought I did."

"What do you mean?"

"Well, I could've dropped the box and let someone else say what was in it. But instead I thought it was all up to me because I was holding the damn box. So welcome to my life, Ruby Tuesday. Freeze in the moment but come up with the perfect solution after the fact."

"That seems pretty normal. I do that all the time."

"But at some point don't you need to be able to figure out your shit when it's happening?"

"Like right now?"

"I wish I had right now figured out." His voice drifts. Like he's trying to solve the mess we're in.

"I can't keep my eyes open, Charlie."

"Rest. It's your turn. I'll try to figure out how to tunnel us out of here using mind control."

"Okay." I close my eyes. I slip.

HANDS

In the space between waking and sleeping, I let my thoughts float to Leo. Fireworks. Hot mochas. Kisses along my collarbone. My earlobe between his teeth.

Then the memory of only him and me. Two days ago. On Thursday. After my practice and before his. Curled up on my bed. My head on his chest. My breathing calm. My arm across his stomach. Content.

Until he pulled my hand to his. Glued us together palm-to-palm.

"Your hands are bigger than mine," he said. I knew he didn't say it to be mean. It was merely an observation. A thought bubble. But it hit me like a kettlebell to my stomach. He tapped his big toe to mine. "Your feet, too."

I untangled myself from his arms and legs and moved to the edge of the bed. I sat with my back to him. He pulled up, put his hands on my shoulders.

"Hey, what is it? What'd I do?"

I felt the tears forming. I hated that I was crying. I pressed them back with the pads of my thumbs. My too-big thumbs.

One day I will meet someone with bigger hands than mine.

"Ruby, talk to me."

"It's nothing. I don't want it to be anything."

"But it is something. Is it about your hands? What is it?" He climbed off the bed, kneeled in front of me. Put his elbows on my knees. He looked up at me open and honest and true. His hair mussed. His big eyes shining. Showing me all the things that made me fall for him.

"You didn't have to say it."

"What?"

"That my hands are bigger."

"But they are." He didn't understand what the problem was. He was just stating facts. No big deal.

"Yes, but you didn't have to make a thing of it."

"I wasn't making a thing of it. I was only saying—"

"You were saying I have bigger hands than you."

"You *do* have bigger hands than me."

I pulled at my hair. He didn't get it. He was saying things without thinking. "I know! But I don't want to!"

"Oh."

"Yeah. *Oh.*"

"I'm sorry. I didn't mean . . ." He pressed his fingertips into my calves, like he needed to have my full attention. "I was just talking. I don't care if your hands are bigger than mine. It doesn't bother me."

"But it bothers *me.*"

"It shouldn't."

"Yeah, yeah. I know it *shouldn't.* We're all supposed to love every freaking thing about ourselves. We're never supposed to have a negative thought. But . . . I don't necessarily *like* my big hands. Or my big feet. Sometimes I hate being six feet tall. And

I know it's so nothing in the grand scheme of things. There are way worse things to feel bad about. But sometimes I wish I didn't stand out."

"But you don't stand out because of your hands and feet or how tall you are."

"So you can honestly say that you never notice my head bobbing inches above everyone else's as I walk down the hallway?"

"Ruby." His fingertips pressed again. "I wish you could know what I think when I see you walking down the hallway." His tone flirted.

I pushed away. "You don't get it."

"No. *You* don't get it." He pulled me closer to the edge of the bed. Stood us up together. Tapped his forehead to mine because we were the same height. "You're the only one I see walking down the hall. Because it's you. And I really like you." He raised my hand to his mouth. Kissed my knuckles. One by one. "A lot."

Until my knees went a little weak. And I pulled him in closer.

"I really like you, too," I said. "But you should probably go now. My mom'll be home soon."

"Okay. But you're not mad, are you?"

"I'm not mad," I said. And I wasn't. But I was *something*. I just didn't know what exactly.

CHAPTER ELEVEN

3:43 A.M.

I HEAR MUFFLED CRIES FOR HELP, SOFT AND far away. They are a whisper. Like bright orange autumn leaves fluttering to the ground. Like the first drops of rain that feel like mist from the spray of the ocean. Like dandelion fluff blown from the bulb.

Too small.

Too light.

Too subtle to even comprehend.

I call for Charlie, but when his coughing starts, I know it wasn't him. The cry was only something my mind made up. There's nobody here but us. That's the reality of this situation. That's the truth of where we are.

The broken walls. The creaking tables. The dark air. The stiff legs. The empty stomachs. The sticky tongues. The dusty eyes. The pee-stained pants.

Charlie mumbles. He says something that sounds like a promise. Rising and falling from his mouth and hitting the ground. His words don't have anywhere to go.

"Who are you talking to?" I say.

"God."

"Oh." That's not what I was expecting.

"What? You're not chatting it up with The Guy in the Sky? Making all your bargains? It's emergency behavior 101, isn't it?"

"No."

"What do you know that I don't?"

"Nothing. I just don't believe in God."

"No?"

"Nope."

"Huh."

"*Huh* isn't the usual response," I say.

"It's unexpected, I guess, but it's all good. I mean, your life, your call, right?" Charlie rustles, attempting to shift positions. "Do you ever worry you're wrong?"

I snort. "Like right now? Do you think I should be worried?" He's silent. Too silent. "Go ahead. You can say it."

"Haven't you thought about what happens next if we don't make it out?" He's letting his pessimism seep in.

"I've thought about it. But prayers never entered my mind."

"I don't get why you sound so defensive."

"I'm tired of explaining myself, I guess."

"No explanation necessary. To be honest, I don't even know why I'm praying. God shouldn't forgive me."

"Charlie, don't."

"It's true, Ruby."

"Charlie, why can I see so clearly that what happened to Jason isn't your fault but you can't?"

"You remembered his name."

"Well, yeah. He was your friend. He's part of your story. He's part of you."

"That's a super-nice way to put it. And I appreciate that. You might want to think about majoring in being rad when you go to college."

"I like hearing you talk about college. Because it means you can imagine the future." But then I realize he didn't talk about himself. He only talked about me and what I should do.

"Sure, Ruby. I can try."

"You don't sound very convincing."

"What do you want me to say here?"

"You don't have to say anything. But, the thing is, you still did. You told me what happened to Jason, and that makes me think there's a part of you that actually wants to talk about it."

"It's easier to talk to you. I don't know you."

"Ouch."

He coughs. "Sorry. I only mean . . . you're not my parents. Or my brother. You didn't walk into this laundromat with any expectations of me besides the hope that I'd buy you beer."

"Which you wouldn't."

"I wouldn't."

"So what will you do?"

"What do you want me to do?"

"I want you to talk to someone who isn't me. Or God. So you're not holding all this guilt inside. I want you to realize God doesn't need to forgive you. *You* need to forgive you."

Charlie is quiet. Thinking. I hope he heard me. Really heard me.

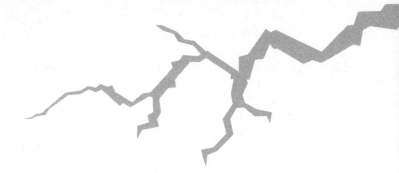

CHAPTER TWELVE

5:00 A.M.

MY SKIN PRICKLES. LIKE THOUSANDS OF TINY bugs have found my body and burrowed into every inch of me. They take up residence in the pinholes of my hair shafts. All over my scalp. Along my right arm. Deep down in the pulsing cut of my left arm. In each millimeter of stubble on my legs. My tongue sticks to the roof of my mouth. My left foot has been asleep and frozen for so long I've forgotten what it feels like. I twist it. Shake. I can't feel it move. I kick again.

Too hard.

Part of this safe space crumbles. I squeeze my eyes shut. Turn my head. Shout. There's nothing I can do. Nowhere I can go to save myself.

"What's happening?!" Charlie yells.

I scream when something falls sideways and lands across my

thighs. My body stills. Waits. I attempt to fathom how broken I am.

"The bottom half of the table fell on me. But there's something else on top of it," I say. If I push it away, everything else could come crashing down. I'll be buried alive.

And then my fingertips hit something wet. Blood? It's soaking my jeans. I suck in a breath, release a yelp.

"Dammit, Ruby! What's going on?" The panic's returned in the rise of his voice.

"I think I'm bleeding."

I don't even hear what Charlie asks me after that. He yells something about my arm but I can't hold on to his words. Everything is numb. I might not be able to feel the pain of being broken. Maybe I'm impaled. Maybe my thighs are ripped open, exposing flesh and bone.

Maybe my mind is blocking out the agony to protect me.

"Ruby!" Charlie's voice is so loud. It's a roar. He's a lion. Ferocious. I'm surprised it doesn't break down these walls. "Are you okay?"

"I don't know."

The wetness keeps coming, stopping in a puddle against my hand. I dip my fingertips. Pull them to my face. Let them linger. Afraid to know. But finally, I bring them to my nose. Sniff. I expect the rust-and-salt smell of blood, but it isn't that. It's something else.

Soap.

I stick my tongue out, brave a taste.

Water.

"Water!" I shout.

It's tinged with the flavor of laundry detergent but it's so diluted I can't imagine there's much of it. I can't feel actual soap bubbles. They aren't popping on my tongue or in my hands. I dip my fingertips into the puddle again. Stick them into my mouth.

I try not to think of the filthy floor because the relief of something wet on my dry tongue and parched throat is too good.

"Water?!" Charlie shouts. "Where?"

"I knocked something over. With my foot. It opened up a space for water from a washing machine. It's a little bit soapy." It's weird to think it might be from the load of towels I was washing. That moment feels so normal and far away now. A time when my biggest problem was my mom dating my coach. I walked into this laundromat trying to find the courage to ask a stranger to buy me beer, and now that stranger is my friend and I'm trying to find the courage to stay alive. Life can change in an instant. With a phone call like my mom got the day my dad was hit by a car. Like yesterday when the earthquake hit. I can't help but rethink what matters and what doesn't. What once felt so big suddenly seems so small.

And things I would've taken for granted, like water, are an enormous gift.

I cup my hand against the stream, suck down what I can get into my mouth, but the rivulet is running away from me fast. My heart races, terrified I'll lose it before I get enough. My hands slap at the ground, collecting as much as I can.

"Ruby. Be careful."

I freeze, my hand across my mouth, suddenly ashamed of my good fortune. Like I never should've spoken of it.

"Why?"

"I don't know. The laundry detergent, maybe?"

"I can barely taste it."

My washing machine was filling up when the earthquake hit. It's mostly water. With traces of soap. But even if it tasted more strongly of soap, I'm not sure I would stop drinking.

"I'm glad you have water," he says, but I can hear the break in his voice. The part I know he doesn't want me to hear.

Why her and not me?

I want to know that, too. Why me and not him?

"Can you move something out of the way?" I say. "To make space for water to get to you?"

"I'm afraid to try. Things are pretty tight here."

But I hear him rustling around. I hear him trying.

"It's not getting to me," he says.

I curve my hand against the puddle, trying to train it to run in Charlie's direction.

"What about now?"

"No."

I adjust my fingers.

The water is ice-cold. I hadn't noticed before. It hits me now. *Too cold to ever be blood.* But it's dangerous, too. Because I'm sitting in a near-freezing puddle of water in the dead of winter.

I lift my hand to my mouth, suck in another swallow.

It goes down my throat along with the guilt and the fear.

What's one more ounce of guilt anyway? I'm already filled with it. I'm such a hypocrite to sit here and tell Charlie to stop feeling guilty when I carry my own around with me everywhere I go. Mila has made sure of it.

FAVORS

We followed the guy with our beer as he marched down the sidewalk toward the beach. Mila seemed fine with the plan. She even seemed into it.

"We have to be at this party," Thea said, scampering behind Mila. "It's my brother's birthday."

Not true. Thea didn't even have a brother.

"I love a party. Where is it?"

I could just see it. The five of us walking into Cody Calabrese's backyard with that guy. Mila and Iris with their skirts. Thea with her hair. Juliette with her smile. Me with my legs. And him. Everyone turning to look at us. Wondering why.

"It's invite only," Juliette said. "Sorry."

He laughed. "What? Like there's actually a list at the door like some exclusive nightclub? I'm sure it'll be fine if I go with you. Are we heading in the right direction?"

"It's in town. We should turn around," I said. I knew it was better to be by lights and cars and people, so at least turning around would get us back there.

"You seriously want to go to the party?" Mila said.

"You seriously want to go to the beach?" I said.

"I seriously want that beer."

"I'll say," Thea murmured.

The guy leaned back, looked us up and down. "Such

indecisive girls. Come on, what's it gonna be? Beach or party? Should we flip a coin?"

"We want to go to the party," Thea said.

"Same." Juliette.

"Yep." Iris.

"Well, I'm going to the beach," Mila said.

"Beach it is." He hoisted the slipping bag of beer up under his arm and hooked his other arm around Mila's shoulders. She actually leaned into him. And I didn't even know what I was watching anymore.

I tried to communicate to Mila with my eyes. *What are you doing? What are you thinking?*

But I knew her focus was only on that bag of beer.

Thea, Iris, and Juliette had already turned around, ready to leave. Until Iris stopped. She asked, "Are you coming, Ruby?"

Mila looked at me. Challenging. Testing our friendship.

I couldn't leave her.

Could I?

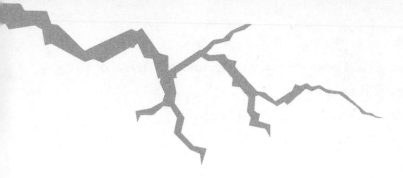

CHAPTER THIRTEEN

7:02 A.M.

LIGHT SHOOTS THROUGH THE CRACK above me.

It's the sun. The sun!

I've been in the dark for so long I forgot light existed. I shut my eyes. Wish for it to warm the frozen tip of my nose, the drenched cold of my thighs. I imagine Hawaii and summertime and a perfect August day. I hear Charlie move in the distance.

"Morning," he says, like an acknowledgment and not a greeting.

"Do you see the sun?"

"One streak. Through a crack by my chest."

Today is so unlike a normal morning in our town. Where the diner across the street from here has a line out the door and the smell of coffee and bacon seeps out to the sidewalk. My teammates and I pass it on our bikes on our way back from morning practice.

Hair wet.

Ugg boots working hard to keep our feet warm. I wish I were wearing them now. I can't even feel my toes anymore.

Sometimes, on Saturdays, we have time to stop. We load up on pancakes. Or scrambled eggs. And we never see the bottoms of our coffee mugs because the waitress tops us off with every other sip.

My stomach growls.

Then sinks.

What if the diner is no longer standing?

What if the fifties-style jukebox is broken? The hand-painted front windows advertising weekly specials shattered? Surely there were people eating there when the earthquake happened.

I think of everywhere I know. All the places in town. The places where my friends could've been. All the ways they could be hurt.

Dying.

Dead.

I would've been in the pool. Surrounded by my team. Would that have been better than being here with Charlie? Would we have survived? Or would we have been scattered like broken toothpicks across the pool deck?

"Do you hear that?" Charlie says.

Not far away there is noise. Shouts. I can't tell what they're saying, but whoever is making the noise is close to us.

My heartbeat kicks up. Hope. They're looking for us.

"Help!" I shout.

Then Charlie: "Over here!"

There is relief in my muscles and bones over the realization that we've been found. Finally. Soft beds. Hot showers. Clean pants. Mountains of food. Help has finally arrived.

There are more hollers farther away.

The screech of a whistle.

"Where are they?!" I yell to Charlie. I try to move in this space. To make myself loud enough.

I need something more.

I reach for my phone. It'll make noise. An alarm. A song from my pregame pump-up playlist. Something loud. Something strong.

Something.

I pull my phone to my face. Tap the screen. Heart hoping. Heart crashing.

There's nothing but fizz.

The water fried it.

The puddle of water I sucked into my mouth from the tips of my fingers to save my life killed my phone.

I don't even have Leo's picture anymore.

Charlie can't even hear me tell him it's gone. He's yelling too loud to hear anything but his own voice. I yell, too. I yell loud and long. Until my throat is as raw and scratchy as it was before I found water. I yell until my voice is nearly lost.

The whistles back off. They push away like a bus from the curb. They didn't come for us. False alarm. They decided nothing's here.

Going.

Going.

Gone.

CHAPTER FOURTEEN

7:21 A.M.

"FUCK!" CHARLIE SHOUTS.

He smacks hard at something in his space. The walls creak. Like a haunted house. And then there's a wobble.

"Stop it! You're going to make everything cave in!"

"I don't fucking care!" He smacks again. Growls. Punches.

There's a crash. I shut my eyes. Hold my breath.

When it stops, he punches again. Another wobble. Another crash.

I cross my hands over my head to protect myself. "Charlie! What's wrong with you? Do you want to kill us?"

"What's the point, Ruby? Might as well make it quick and painless. Nobody's coming for us, okay? Do you think rescue's going to get any closer than it just did?"

"Charlie," I whimper. "You're scaring me. Please don't do this. I need you to be brave for me. Please."

"Shut up, Ruby. It's done. Face it."

His anger slices me wide open. I don't even know this person. But maybe I never knew Charlie at all.

I'm angry, too. My whole body shakes with the force of it. But I'm not ready for these walls to come crashing down yet. I don't want to stop hoping. My elbow and my hip bone grind into the hard floor underneath me. It hurts to even move my left arm now. It's so hot. Puffy. Oozing. And the rest of my skin is already worn down, rubbed raw and chafed, drawing blood.

So maybe hope is useless.

Maybe all of my flesh will fall right off of me until I'm nothing but a heap of bones. I'll be a pile of myself underneath whatever Charlie makes crash down on top of us.

I'll die here.

I thought my dad was young when he died, but I'm thirteen years younger than he was. There is so much living I'll never do. I won't move into a dorm or play water polo in college. I won't backpack across Europe like my mom did or make new friends in countries far away from home. Or see the friends I miss so badly it cracks my heart open. I'll never again drive a car with the windows down and the moonlight bright. Or eat chocolate. Or float in the ocean. Or ski down a mountain.

I'll never hug my mom.

I'll never breathe in the gardenia-and-lemonade smell of her.

I'll never hear her full-bellied, head-tilting, hair-falling-out-of-her-ponytail laugh again.

I'll never see my room. Or home.

I'll never kiss Leo.

There is nothing else after this. Just dirt. A laundromat grave. Flesh falling off my bones.

"Do it," I say. "Punch it again. Get it over with."

On the other side of me there's only a heavy breath drawn in deep.

"Shit, Ruby," Charlie murmurs. "I'm sorry. I'm so sorry. You're all I have here. I'm losing it. Please don't be mad at me."

I can't be mad. Because I understand. I do.

Pessimism lives here now.

It's breaking both of us.

"I'm not mad," I say. "Maybe you're right."

"Don't say that. This can't be how it happens."

"But isn't that how it is? One second you're folding laundry and the next second you're diving under a table in the middle of an earthquake."

"One minute you're hanging out at a fraternity house like any other Friday night, the next minute someone's calling nine-one-one." He punches at something again, and it creaks. "What's the point?"

"The point is that you try. You tried that night. You're trying now."

"But why am I trying?"

"Because you can never stop trying, Charlie. You can never stop trying to fight for what you believe in or what you want out of life. Everything is connected. One thing leads to the next. It all matters."

CONNECTIONS

People not in the know seem to think swimmers and water polo players are basically the same thing simply because both sports fall under the umbrella of aquatics.

They aren't the same.

In my experience, swimmers and water polo players hardly even hang out with each other. That's probably why I hadn't known a whole lot about Leo other than the fact that he'd held our school's record in the two-hundred-yard individual medley and the one-hundred-yard fly. I'd known only because the school paper plastered his name all over the sports section every week during swim season. But on the first night we hung out together after the Fourth of July, I also learned Leo held California state records and wanted to swim in college as much as I wanted to play water polo. He was already being courted by Division I schools and was hoping to get scholarship money as well.

It certainly felt like he'd earned such an opportunity after I heard his workout schedule. It was way more intense than mine for water polo. He went from five to seven a.m., Monday through Friday. Plus he worked out for two hours with the school's swim team in the afternoon during the three months of swim season and, twice a week, two more hours with his club swim team in the evening. His weekend schedule varied depending on meets, but, in general, he worked out twice a day on Saturdays and had Sundays off.

Leo lived to swim.

"And I thought I was made up of fifty percent chlorine," I said as I wound my chopsticks through the sheen of my ramen broth, creating a kind of eddy so my noodles would be more secure before I slurped them into my mouth. We'd gone to a restaurant by the mall so we could see a movie after. It was a lot for someone with Leo's schedule to pack into one night. "How are you even here right now? How are you awake?"

He gathered his noodles with his chopsticks. "I really wanted to be here so . . . I planned ahead."

"What do you mean?"

"I swam for three hours this morning instead of two so I'd only have to do one hour this evening. That way, I could go to dinner with you. And a movie. Plus it's summer. I got to take a nap."

"I'm flattered?"

He laughed. "Good."

"But wait." I set my chopsticks across the top of my bowl and studied him. "I don't remember you sneaking off for swim practice on the Fourth of July. Did I miss something?"

"Well, yeah. It was a national holiday. I get national holidays off."

"So you're like a mail carrier."

He laughed. "Pretty much. They're the ones with that motto

about delivering letters through rain or sleet or snow or blazing hot sun, right?"

"Yeah. Something like that."

"Might as well be a swim motto."

"Polo, too." I felt such camaraderie in that moment. Like Leo was someone who would always understand me. "Actually, no. Polo is only twice a day." I added up the hours in my head. "You spend six hours in the pool some days. That's brutal."

"I only do the triple workouts during high school swim season." He added some heat to his ramen by taking a spoonful of rayu from the metal jar at the edge of the table. "Otherwise it's only twice a day."

"Can I ask you something?"

He mixed the chili oil into his broth with his chopsticks. "I think so."

"Why even bother with the school swim team? It's not like they're that good. Why not just focus on club?"

"Now you sound like my parents. Have you been talking to them? Conspiring against me?" He smiled.

"Nope. I promise." I crossed my heart.

He took a sip of water. "I look at swim team like it's the one thing I can do to feel like I'm part of something at school. Otherwise, I'm only there for classes." He bit into his soft-boiled egg. Chewed. Swallowed. "I mean, I guess I could run for ASB or something, but I don't exactly have the time. Swimming is something I'm good at, so why not just do that?

And then I can actually feel like I'm having a sliver of a high school experience."

"That makes sense." And then, "So not much of a social life for you, huh?"

"Not a stellar one." He grinned at me. "But I'm hoping it just got better."

CHAPTER FIFTEEN

9:00 A.M.

I PULL THE HOOD FROM MY DAMP SWEAT-shirt over my face. Talk to Charlie with my eyes shut. The sleeve covers the cut on my left arm, and I beg for the wet cold of it to tame the fire carving a crevice through my skin.

It doesn't.

I push at the heat. Suck in a breath. "Can my arm fall off from infection?"

"No."

"But maybe?"

"You're fine, Ruby."

"They could have to amputate it. To save my life. What if someone has to saw it off to even get me out of here?"

I'd have to go to a hospital. I hate hospitals. Hospitals are where people go to die.

"If cutting off injured body parts is the only way out, they'll have to saw me in half. So count your blessings." He coughs. "Think you could talk about something else?"

"Like what?"

"You said your mom's dating your coach. That sounds salacious."

"More like weird."

"You don't like him?"

"I like him fine. I just don't like him dating my mom. Except . . ."

"Except what?"

"Nothing. Forget it."

"Nope. Can't forget it now. You already started it."

"It's weird, isn't it? How things that seemed like such a big deal yesterday don't matter as much today? Like if my mom and my coach showed up right now, I'd probably throw them a wedding."

"I'd eat all the cake."

I think about the things I was worried about before the earthquake. My mom and Coach. Finding a dress for the water polo banquet. AP tests in May.

"So much doesn't matter anymore," I say.

"I know what you mean. I guess now we have to decide what still matters."

There's something. Mila. And that's a big thing.

"My friend has a drinking problem. I'm afraid she's going to end up like your friend."

He shuffles. Something creaks. We stay still. Wait for quiet.

"The one on your team? Who lost her ring in Hawaii?"

"Yeah. Mila. I understand you more than you know, Charlie. I just kept everything about Mila to myself, and she ended up in a lot of trouble because of it."

"What kind of trouble?"

"The kind of trouble people with drinking problems get into. The kind of trouble friends want to be able to fix, but it's too big. Too much."

"Yeah, I'm familiar with that kind of trouble."

"I know you are."

"I'm sorry," he says. "I'm sorry you're going through that. And I'm sorry for your friend."

"Me too."

I can hope I'll get out of here and Mila's okay and we'll be okay. I can hope she wants to try.

FRIENDS

The beach was windy, and the cold of the sand seeped through the back of my jeans. I was holding a can of beer, waiting for Leo to text me back, and watching Mila run around, singing some annoying song about counting stars at the top of her lungs. Beer sloshed out from the can she was tipping sideways when she tripped and fell into the guy, giggling and patting his chest.

Turned out his name was Robert.

"Ooh," she said, smoothing her hand across Robert's chest. "You're hard." She tittered. "I mean . . . here." She patted his pecs.

He shook his head. Smiled. Then dipped her, like he was all romantic and was going to kiss her, but she lost her balance and toppled to the ground. Robert hovered above her like a shadow, offering to help her up. Mila slapped at his hand, laughing.

I walked over to them. Mila came up to his armpit when she was standing, but I was as tall as him. Mila grabbed my hand.

"Come count the stars with me," she said, pulling me to the ground. Her wobbly grip made me stumble, and I landed on top of her.

"Well, all right," Robert said, grinning down at us. "Three is always more fun."

He angled in.

Breathed his breath.

I scrambled up. Moved back.

He laughed, pushing forward. He pinched my waist. "Oh, come on. I like a big girl who doesn't need me to be gentle."

I spun away. Put up my hands. "Don't touch me. Ever."

Mila stood. Swayed. Squinted.

Competed.

She grabbed Robert's hand and pulled him behind her toward the sand dunes. Shouted, "Ruby already has a boyfriend."

I hated her right then.

I paced. Rolled my hands into fists. I wanted to punch something. But I felt so helpless. He touched me without my permission. What was he going to do to her?

But maybe she actually liked him. Maybe she was good with it. She invited him here. She pulled him behind the dunes.

No.

She was too drunk.

I needed to check in with her.

I brushed off my jeans and headed to the dunes.

"Mila!" I shouted to let her know I was coming.

I rounded the sand dune where she was giggling and swatting at Robert, who was nuzzling her neck.

"Stop," she murmured, and that's all I needed to hear.

"We should go," I said. I walked around them and pulled at Mila's hand.

She giggled.

"Are you fighting over me now? You're always so jealous, Ruby."

"Hey, hey, hey," Robert said, pulling Mila toward him. "I don't think your friend is ready to go." *Friend.* He didn't use her name. Wanted to keep her anonymous.

"She said stop."

"She didn't mean it." He looked at Mila. "Right, beautiful?"

He angled his body over hers, trying to ease her back into the sand.

Mila's eyes went wide, and she squeezed my hand. Tried to use me for leverage to roll out from under him. But he was big. And strong. And not giving in.

"Actually"—she sounded out of breath as she pushed on his chest—"Ruby's right. We need to go." She tried to twist away, but she was wedged between him and the sand.

She looked at me. Eyes pleading. *Help.*

I grabbed her hand. Pulled hard. Her shoulder nailed Robert on the chin.

He bolted up, sending sand flying. "Are you kidding me right now?"

"I think I'm gonna throw up," Mila said, scrambling away. Heaving. "Ruby," she whimpered, "hold my hair."

She shoved her hand out to me, opening and closing it, fluttering her fingers, wanting me to grab them. I didn't.

"We're good here," I said to Robert, standing tall and squaring my shoulders. "You should go. I'm pretty sure she's done for the night."

Robert grabbed my arm, digging his fingers in tight. "What about you? Are you done?" My heart skittered in my chest. Breath stuck in my throat. I was too frozen with fear to move.

"Ruuuuuuuuby," Mila whimpered. She stood up, teetering like a newborn colt.

Robert looked at me. Looked at her. Finally loosened his grip. Pushed me toward Mila.

I gathered her hair into my fist right before she lunged forward and threw up into the sand.

"Unreal," he said, walking away. "Happy fucking New Year."

CHAPTER SIXTEEN

11:33 A.M.

I WOULD GIVE ANYTHING FOR A RUNNY NOSE.
My mucous membranes are cracked. My sinuses sting. My throat feels like I swallowed a handful of sand. I can actually imagine my teeth crunching down on the bits and pieces of it and wincing as it goes down, cutting up my insides along the way.

I dream of snot and postnasal drip.

How disgusting is that? This is what I've become. This is how dried out and cracked I am.

Even my tongue hurts. It stays stuck to the roof of my mouth like it's coated with paste. The sides of it tingle, like when your feet and hands fall asleep. I try to stretch it by rolling it from one side of my mouth to the other. My lips smack and stick. The skin on my body burns with cracks and fissures. My arm is agony. The heat. The heartbeat.

And I'm cold. Shivering in this damp puddle of water.

I can't check my phone to know what time it is. But a whole day has to have passed at least.

How many days can I go? How long will it be before I cave in on myself? Before I'm a dusty heap of nothing?

"I don't think I'm okay, Charlie." I try to twist my limp neck, but it's almost too hard to lift my head.

Charlie shifts. Groans from the effort. "Negativity like that is not allowed here, Ruby. We're getting out. And when we do, we'll be friends."

Not strangers. Friends.

"Promise?"

"I'm holding up my fist for you to bump."

"Bump."

He sucks in a breath. "I really am going to come watch you play water polo, so be ready. I'll bring one of those giant foam fingers to your games to embarrass you. And after you win we'll go to a taco stand by the beach and I'll ask you a million questions because I still won't understand anything about how to play."

"No way. I'll make you an expert in no time. I'll make you get in the pool. Teach you how to eggbeater." I manage a laugh. "And then I'll bring a foam finger to your poetry readings. Or when I watch your films. Or go to your art shows. Would that be tacky?"

"Please do it. I love tacky."

I have to hold on to being able to see these things. Because time is passing us by now. And nobody is coming.

I haven't peed since the middle of the night.

My mouth is sticky.

My stomach is empty.

My body can't move.

My skin doesn't feel like skin. It sags. Like a swimsuit drip-drying on the balcony railing. I don't feel like me.

I'm done.

My thoughts are slipping.

How long before I'm gone?

DONE

I pulled Mila's car up to the curb in front of her house and rolled down the windows because the front seat smelled vaguely of beer and barf. Creeper Robert was long gone, and Mila sat stoically, not wanting to look at me, so I looked at the oak tree in the front yard instead. It still had the tree house her dad built tucked up in its branches. We spent hours there in elementary school, inventing secret codes and playing with our Polly Pocket dolls. By middle school, it turned into a place of refuge when her parents were fighting. It was a relief once her dad moved into his own condo across town because Mila could trade the tree house for her bedroom. She lived with her mom Monday through Friday but stayed with her dad on the weekends and certain holidays.

"Wait. Aren't you supposed to go to your dad's tonight?"

"I am. But I'm not. Obviously."

Her house was dark. Not even the porch light was on. "Is your mom even home? I can take you to your sister's."

"No, thank you. Her loser boyfriend's staying over and—" She shuddered. "Just no."

"Well, won't your dad freak out if you don't come home?"

"Sure. If he comes home."

"So you're trying to piss him off? Is that what's wrong tonight? Is it about the divorce?"

She rolled her eyes. "That would solve everything in your head, wouldn't it? Poor Mila, all messed up because her mommy and daddy don't love each other anymore." Her neck lolled to the side as she focused on me. "I'm fine."

"You don't seem fine. I'm worried about you."

"Don't."

"Don't what? Worry?"

She blew her bangs off her forehead. *"Don't* anything right now. Please."

"Did you really want to hang out with that Robert guy tonight?"

"So what if I did?"

"I just want to understand. Is it so important to get drunk that you'll go off with anyone who'll buy you beer?"

"You went too." She looked out the window instead of at me. At a streetlight flickering on and off one house down. "You could've gone to Cody's with everyone else. You could've left me with Robert."

"I wouldn't have done that. I needed to go with you."

"Why? I didn't exactly handcuff you and take you with me."

This was typical Mila. The Queen of Twist.

"I wouldn't have left you because I'm not that kind of friend. And I think you know that. It's why you make sure I'm always there. Because you know I'll bail you out of whatever mess you get yourself into."

She looked at me, eyes glazed over. Hair stuck to the side of her head. Mascara streaks dripping. "Whatever."

I pounded the steering wheel. "Not *whatever*. It's a big deal. What if we hadn't gotten away tonight? What if I'd hurt that guy and ended up in trouble? Or what if he'd hurt me? That's not what a real friend would want for another friend. I don't want *you* to get hurt. That's why I always go with you. And now I want to help you, but I don't know what's going on. I don't know why you want to numb yourself every weekend. You can talk to me, you know. Or I'll go with you somewhere. To talk to someone else. Or to go to an AA meeting or something. Just say you'll go." She wouldn't look at me, but she also didn't open the car door, so I spilled all the words I'd been holding inside. "I don't know what to do anymore. You want me to look out for you, but you don't even want to look out for yourself."

"Ugh. You're so dramatic. Are you breaking up with me?" She snort-laughed.

I realized how true that was. How done I was. "Basically, yeah."

"So let me get this straight. You're up in my face about me being a shitty friend but you're the one deciding not to hang out anymore."

Queen. Of. Twist.

"Mila, at some point, I can't do it anymore. For me. But also for you. I can't be your safety net over and over again. If you want to talk about getting help, I'll go. I'll be there for that. But I can't be there anymore for the kind of shit that happened tonight."

"Stop. I can quit anytime. I'm just having fun. You're making way too much out of this." She opened her door and stumbled out onto the sidewalk. "We're done here. But go ahead and take my car home. Because a real friend wouldn't want you walking alone this late at night."

She was being sarcastic, and that was the whole problem.

She'd never get it. Or take responsibility. Not until something really bad happened. And all I could do was hope it wouldn't be too late when it did.

It wasn't midnight by that point. But an old year was about to creep into a new one. I made the choice then. I wouldn't spend the next year the way I'd spent the last one.

I was done with Mila.

CHAPTER SEVENTEEN

1:01 P.M.

THE EARTH IS A TOTAL JERK RIGHT NOW.
It bucks beneath me, like a bull in a rodeo, as another after-shock hits. Not that I've ever actually ridden a bull. I've never even been to a rodeo. I've only seen them in movies or read about them in books. There are a million things I haven't seen. Haven't done.

Charlie whimpers.

"Hold on," I say.

"To what?"

Charlie is speaking literally. I'm speaking figuratively. But what's the point? What's even left to hold on to?

"Just hold on!" I say, because it's easier to repeat myself than explain myself.

I cover my head with my hands.

The table legs creak around me. I can't look. I pull my hoodie in tighter over my face. Bits of crumbling cement hit my hands, pounding my knuckles to a bloody pulp.

I hear something crash.

"Argh!" Charlie. He's getting pummeled.

The earth bucks again. Bigger. Stronger.

Thumps.

Grinds.

Charlie is grunts and moans.

And still it goes. Rocking relentlessly. Shaking sharply.

Crumbling. Cracking. Creaking.

I shut my eyes, thinking it can't go on for much longer.

Until, finally, it stops.

"Charlie?" I call through the crack of air above my face. The dust dances around in its light.

"It fell—on me—again—"

"What?"

"The table—and whatever—was on top of it. The dryer, I think. It's—on me again. It pushed the table down. On my chest. There's glass. Cement. I can't"—a grunt—"move it."

I close my eyes. I want to be one of those people who suddenly develops superhuman strength, busts through the walls, and gets us out of here. How can it be that my safe space is almost completely intact but Charlie is pinned again?

Why him and not me?

"Listen to me, Charlie. You did it once. You have to do it again."

"I could still feel my arms before. I still had some strength. My energy is gone."

"You have to move it. Do you hear me?"

He mumbles something to himself, and then the sound of scraping metal echoes. Inch by inch by inch it goes.

Charlie pants.

"You've got this." I try to sound calm, like Coach does when we're down by a point in the last minutes of the fourth quarter and we draw an ejection on the other team to give us a miraculous six-on-five advantage. Yelling doesn't help in that situation. Only confidence does.

Charlie pauses. Breathes in. Breathes out. Grunts. Pushes again. The metal hisses along with him.

"Fuuuuuuuuuuuck!" he shouts. The noise of scraping metal stops, and all that's left is the sound of Charlie's labored breathing.

I can only hear air going out. Not in.

And then the earth shakes again. Harder and stronger than it did a few minutes ago, but only for a moment.

"Charlie!"

He doesn't answer with real words. It's only the sound of something guttural. "Muargh." Like there is a rumble inside of him. Fluids bubbling up.

I reach for him. Spread out my fingers, trying to make them longer. Trying to make contact so he knows he's not alone. So I know I'm not alone.

Then another crash.

"The wall—" Charlie's words get cut.

There is only sound.

It's one thing, then another. Toppling over. Caving in. I imagine that whole side of the laundromat coming down on him. Washers. Dryers. What's left of the ceiling and the walls. All of it collapsing and burying Charlie underneath.

I brace for it to bury me.

"Help!" I shout, even though nobody can. And then I'm whimpering Charlie's name over and over again.

Charlie is blergs and bubbles when the cave-in stops. Gurgles sputtering out of him. A mumbled prayer.

"Jesus." And "God." And "Amen."

I pull my hands back. Hold them to my stomach, trying to keep myself from being sick. Because when I call his name again, there is only silence.

QUIET

A whisper.
An afghan blanket.
The breeze on my face.
The sun on my closed eyelids.
My mom's hands.
Leo's hair.
My bedroom at dawn.
Empty Christmas stockings.
SAT testing.
Sunday morning.
Twinkle lights on our back patio.
Birthday candles going dim.
Marshmallows melting into hot chocolate.
Steam rising over the swimming pool at night.
The shuffle of papers.
The scratch of pencils writing in-class essays.
The front seat of the car without the radio on.
Rose petals in my neighbor's garden.
The first drizzle of rain.
The last tears falling.
Charlie.

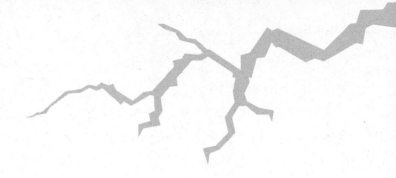

CHAPTER EIGHTEEN

2:38 P.M.

I CAN'T STOP MYSELF FROM CALLING Charlie's name through the cold, dusty air. I am a whisper. A plea.

He doesn't answer.

I convince myself he's only sleeping. Happily dreaming of things he loves.

I should be quiet. I should let him dream.

I want to sleep, too, but I need to stay awake. And aware. In case someone comes. I listen for a shout. A whistle. A siren. Hope.

California has to have been declared a national disaster by now. The Big One could have cut off the water supply and gutted entire towns. It could leave a death toll in the thousands. It could have crushed buildings and split freeways in half. Rescue crews would be everywhere. Help would have come in from other states. People and emergency medical supplies and blood-bank donations would arrive.

I know what I've seen on TV of disasters in other places. Of hurricanes in the South. Of tornadoes in the Midwest. Of earthquakes in other countries. My brain is a swirl of images of what those towns looked like and what those people had to do. If here and now is anything like that, then people are helping somewhere. There might be rescue stations set up with donations of water and diapers and tampons and oversize sweatshirts. There might even be one right down the street from here. I picture myself arriving there. Shuffling in on dragging feet. I'd come in slow motion, my own version of the zombie apocalypse. There will be first aid tents and doctors with gentle hands and soothing voices to help me. And they'll find my mom. And Leo.

"Charlie," I whisper again. Only wishing. I am breath and hope.

I am things I cannot say.

I am words not spoken out loud.

LOUD

The stands at a final water polo game.

My neighbor's dog when the mailman arrives.

Mila's car radio as we drive to the beach with the windows down.

The whistle of the train as it rolls through the industrial park.

A locker room full of pumped-up girls after a playoff win.

The low-battery warning of the smoke alarm at three a.m.

Fireworks.

Local news helicopters hovering overhead.

New Year's Eve countdowns.

Three. Two. One.

Marching bands in parades.

My favorite band onstage for an encore.

A protest.

A pep rally.

That moment at graduation when everyone throws their caps into the air.

My neighbor's motorcycle.

My other neighbor's drum kit.

Lawn mowers and leaf blowers too early on Sunday mornings.

Downtown.

Freeway traffic.

Me.

CHAPTER NINETEEN

11:58 P.M.

I LET OUT A SCREAM THAT DOESN'T SOUND
human. I slap my hands at this muddled mess. I would toss and
turn and kick and punch if I could move. Instead every inch of me
clenches in anger. Fists folded. Eyes scrunched. Teeth mashing.
Head popping. I scream like a person in the middle of nowhere.
And then I scream for my friend. I just met Charlie, but trust
grows faster in crisis. We told each other things we'd never told
another person. Now he's someone I know almost as well as I
know myself.

Someone I *knew.*

"Charlie!" I shout.

There isn't an answer. There's nothing.

But still I shout. Because it's all I have.

Now that I don't have Charlie.

He stays quiet. He doesn't hear me.

He can't.

I suck in air. I can't get it into my lungs. Quick. Quicker. I inhale. Exhale faster.

I can't breathe.

I can't breathe.

I can't breathe.

Why him and not me?

Fate isn't fateful. Fate is fickle.

The world brings people together in the strangest ways, making us know things we might've missed on ordinary days. Letting us see kindness. Letting us be kind. Too much of life is getting from one thing to the next without stopping to make new connections. We don't slow down enough to get out of our own heads and realize the person next to us might be struggling with big things, too. Bigger things.

I've devoted too much effort to worrying about the smaller things. Like my mom and Coach Sanchez. Or what Leo said about my hands. Or acne! For crying out loud, the amount of time I have spent worrying about a zit . . . And for what? It's the big things that matter. Because the world can change in an instant. People die. My mom knows this. Charlie knew it, too. And now I know it as well.

I think of the way I saw Charlie before. The tiny surface things I glimpsed in the minutes before I knew him. His paint-stained knuckles. His perfectly folded T-shirts. The confident way he walked, all artistic in khaki pants. The way he nodded his head of faded blond hair to say hey. The way he wrote in his journal. And then I think of the way I knew him after. The jokes he made. The way he talked to me and kept me from losing hope. I think of the guilt he carried. *The guilt.* Charlie died before he could forgive himself.

It's not supposed to be this way. Charlie is supposed to get out of here. Make amends. He's supposed to live his life.

How long until death comes for me, too? Will it be another aftershock, or will it be something far worse? Starvation? Dehydration? Flesh-eating bacteria? My organs shutting down? A slow, painful progression of things? Will I be too delirious to even understand what's happening, or will I be in excruciating pain?

Was Charlie lucky to go quickly? Is waiting for death the hard part? How long will it take? How long do I have to wait?

And what if Charlie is the only reason I've stayed alive this long?

Without him, who will shout my name when I sleep too deep and too long? Now that he's gone, nobody is here to wake me up to remind me to breathe.

To remind me to live.

My hand is a fist above my face. I move it to stretch my fingers.

And when I do, I notice something.

Wait.

The rubble above me gives. I slide it aside. Push my whole hand through a hole that's a little bigger than my fist. Something shifted. Something changed.

There is space.

I reach through the darkness. Push again. Out and through. I wave my hand around in the empty air. Swat at the open space around it.

"Help!" I shout into the emptiness. My hand swings this way and that even though I know I'm alone in the dark.

But now there is this space. This opening.

This hope.

I pat around it. Gently at first. Quiet. Soft.

Careful.

When I realize it seems to have some give, I begin to claw.

DAY THREE

SUNDAY

CHAPTER TWENTY

12:33 A.M.

I PUNCH TWO FISTS THROUGH THE HOLE I'VE created, but it's still not big enough to get my body through. I open and close my hands. Grasp at empty air. I'm still afraid I might hit glass shards or sharp metal protrusions that are ready and waiting to slice me wide open. Leave me bleeding. Slowly dying.

I shift in my space. Feel the ache in my legs that have been still for too long. I imagine myself unfurling. I reach farther. Catch the lick of a cold breeze on my fingers. I cup my hand against it. The air feels endless. The space infinite. Cleaner. Crisper. Even though it's still pitch-dark in the middle of the night, I want to be in it. I wave my arm around until my hand catches on the table that was once on top of me. Can I move it? I grip the edge with both hands and shove with all my strength, grunting through gritted teeth. My head throbs and my face heats with the effort. My muscles scream like when I push myself doing reps in the weight room. Every inch pulsating.

I'm so tired. I have to breathe for a second.

Pant, pant, pant.

I push again because I have no other choice. I push as the veins in my temples pop and throb in protest.

"Help," I whimper to nobody but the empty air and Charlie's last breath.

I remember water polo hell week and doing eggbeater in the middle of the deep end, hoisting my hands above my head. My arms were like noodles, ready to give out, but still I moved. I wouldn't sink. I wouldn't stop. I would never ever be the first one out of the pool.

I won't give up now. I'm in the pool, my arms aching as if I'm balancing gallon jugs of water above my head. I won't stop pushing. I can't stop until I'm out of here. Sweat drips into my eyes. My heart pounds like it might burst from my chest.

Still I push.

Another shove and something shifts.

Then a crash.

I tuck my chin to my chest, clench my fists, close my eyes, and wait for it.

CHAPTER TWENTY-ONE

1:11 A.M.

WHEN THE TEETERING STOPS I GO BACK
to digging.

I do it for my mom. For Coach and his pep talks. For Leo by
the pool gate. For my teammates. For the hope of mending things
with Mila. For Charlie.

Then suddenly a slash through the palm of my hand. Deep
and instant. I pull it back toward me, crying out as the blood
oozes, seeping until it coats the wristband of my sweatshirt. I push
against the cut with my elbow from my other arm. I don't have
time for injuries.

I pull the wrists of my sweatshirt over my hands, punch my
fists back through the hole, and continue to dig. Nobody else is
going to do this for me. If I don't get myself out of here, I'll end
up like Charlie.

I move my legs again, try to bend my knees, but there's not enough room. I need to get my head through that opening. My knees scrape against the rubble above me, but I'm able to scoot up a few inches. I want to see if I can get my head free, but it's still too dark. I can't see. I don't know what's waiting to drop on me. I don't know what could happen if I try to push myself out now.

It kills me to know I have to wait. Because all the work I've done could be ruined by another aftershock. But I need more light. I need to be able to see so I don't hurt myself.

I pull my head down. Curl into myself on the ground. Whimpering. Hoping against hope that another aftershock doesn't send everything crashing down on top of me again. Ruining the work I've done. Burying me. I tell myself I'll rest for a moment. I'll fill my head with memories until the half-hearted sunlight of dawn arrives.

MIDNIGHT

Once Mila was inside, I checked the clock in her car.
11:40 p.m.

If I hurried, I could still get to Leo before midnight. So I could kiss him. Make New Year's Eve worth something after all. Make that night matter. I texted him. Told him I was on my way.

He texted back. *Where have you been?*

I'll tell you when I see you.

There were cars parked up and down the block, plus a tangle of beach cruiser bikes in the front yard of Cody Calabrese's house when I walked up. Music seeped out onto the street, the same radio station I listened to on Mila's crappy car radio on my way over, playing a countdown of the top one hundred pop songs of the last year. I checked my phone.

11:57 p.m.

It wasn't midnight yet. I could still find Leo. I could still save the night.

I pushed through the wrought-iron gate. Scanned the crowd. The backyard was filled wall-to-wall with people from school. It might as well have been a hallway crammed with lockers and seniors and school dance flyers.

11:58 p.m.

I weaved my way through the cold wintry air that smelled

of campfire smoke and pine needles. I spotted Thea, Iris, and Juliette sharing the hammock, gently pushing themselves back and forth, waiting for midnight. Sitting there with them would've been so much easier than what I had done that night.

"Leo?" I mouthed.

Iris pointed across the pool. I saw him on the deck. Tall and sure, wearing worn jeans and a hoodie and checkerboard Vans. Holding on to a can of Coke. Surrounded by friends. He threw his head back and laughed at something.

His happiness made my tension melt away.

The pool lights were on and the water glowed turquoise at his feet, casting slippery shadows against the wall behind him. He looked like he was underwater. Like I'd have to swim to get to him.

11:59 p.m.

He turned. Saw me. Grinned a grin that lit up his whole face. It lit up the whole backyard.

I wanted to tell him everything and nothing at all.

He rounded the pool. Met me in the middle of the grass. Around us, everyone counted down to midnight, sending streamers flying and party horns bleating.

Leo pressed his mouth to mine at exactly midnight.

I went loose in his arms with relief.

Letting go of the whole night. Of Mila and Robert and beer and the beach.

"You made it," Leo said.

"I made it."

CHAPTER TWENTY-TWO

6:05 A.M.

IT FEELS LIKE I'VE BEEN WAITING FOR DAY- light forever. Hours have surely passed since I initially stuck my hands through the hole. But finally, the first specks of morning light hit my face, warming my nose and cheeks.

I pull from the small well of strength still left in me. Manage to push myself up again. And then I poke my head out. I've barely got enough room. I want to be able to pull my whole body out, but I can't. I look around. You'd never know this was a laundromat if not for the washers and dryers. The walls and doorway have been hollowed out, everything collapsed and broken. Metal. Glass. Concrete. Dust and dirt. I see the road through the shattered window and crushed cars aban-doned in the middle of the street. Collapsed buildings. Buckled asphalt. Above me, half of the roof of the laundromat is gone.

A blue sky and puffy clouds hover overhead. Looking up, the world seems the same. I can almost pretend nothing has changed. I lean back and pretend I'm gazing up at the sky in the middle of that beach in Hawaii that Charlie helped me imagine one time.

"Feel it," he'd said. "Smell it. Like you're there. Like you're home."

I take a moment to pretend. But then I have to return to where I am. Where the rubble is concrete and heavy and I'm not sure how to free myself.

And then I spot it.

Charlie's hand.

A glimpse of his wrist.

Poking out from the rubble.

His bloodied knuckles.

The blue streaks of paint on his fingernails.

I suck in a breath and use my shoulder to push against the hole enough to get my arm through. It scrapes up and down from my shoulder to my fingertips, everything too tight. Too sharp. But I can't care. I won't. All this time, when I kept reaching for Charlie, I couldn't.

But I see how close he is now.

How close he was.

I've spent so much time digging that I can barely breathe. My lungs are full of dust, and it hurts to suck in air. Still, I wiggle. I roll. I push and shove until I have enough room to get my other arm out. I'm twisted sideways on my back with my head outside of the hole and my arms above my head. I need leverage. Something to give me purchase or pull me free.

My eyes dart. Frantic. They snag on rubble and metal and dust and dirt.

But then. Charlie's hand again.

I reach for him. Grasp his hand to help me. It's cold and his fingers don't tangle with mine the way I want them to. I've longed for that contact for hours. Days. To know I didn't make him up in my head. To know I wasn't alone.

I summon up the last ounce of strength I have to pull myself free. And when I'm finally all the way out, I collapse.

Exhausted.

Panting.

Sweating.

I'm a fish pulled from the sea, struggling for breath on the hardwood planks of the pier.

I'm still holding Charlie's hand. The only part of him I can see. I take in the massive pile of debris that's buried him. The blocks of cement. The steel wall of triple-load dryers. Piled up. Pressing down. Against his chest. Making it so hard to breathe. But he managed to get one hand out, the fingernails worn down and bloodied.

Was he digging?

Was he trying to get himself free so he could get me free?

Was he reaching for me the way I was reaching for him?

Could he feel the warm rays of sunlight on his fingers? Is that how he was keeping track of day and night?

I want to pull Charlie from the rubble. Take him with me. But everything is too heavy. I'd find the strength if I thought there was a reason. But I'm holding Charlie's hand in mine and I know what he is.

Cold.

Dead.

Still. I remember my promise.

I work the championship ring from my finger. It doesn't slide right off. I have to twist and turn it. Pull it free. And when it finally comes loose, it almost goes flying, lost to the rubble forever. But I manage to catch it. Grip it. Not let go. I slide it down Charlie's finger, twisting it past the knuckle on his pinkie. It almost looks like it belongs there.

My vision blurs. I swipe at my face, wet with tears. For Charlie.

My friend.

I want to leave something that will tell whoever finds him who he is. But I'm slumping. Slipping. Going under. Until I catch the handles of Charlie's duffel bag. *C. Smith* stenciled on the side. I drag it to me. Rest his hand on top. Hoping this will be enough. The bag slips open, its zipper already undone. Charlie's journal peeks out. The gold stenciled letters across the front. *C. Smith.* Charlie's words are inside it. I can't leave them behind for a stranger to read. Or worse yet, throw away without caring. He deserves better than that. I promised him.

I grab the journal.

Zip it up inside my sweatshirt.

Safe against my heart.

I have to go.

I crawl, dragging my legs behind me as I claw my way out of here. My arm burns with blinding pain. My fingernails are ragged from the digging, some of them torn all the way off and bleeding. The palms of my hands are worn raw and bleeding, too.

And my mind is slipping.

So tired.

So done.

But I'm almost to the blown-out doorway. I'm almost to the parking lot. I'm almost where someone can see me. I don't know how far outside I get when it feels like I can't move anymore. Like I'm literally anchored here. I hoist my arms in front of me. Settle my head on the bent elbow of my good arm.

I just need a minute to catch my breath.

I just need a minute to feel my legs.

I just need a minute to close my eyes.

I just need a minute.

A minute.

A MINUTE

Sixty seconds.
 Fifty seconds.
Forty seconds.
Thirty seconds.
Twenty seconds.
Ten weeks.
Nine is my cap number.
Eight teammates on the bench.
Seven starting players.
Six-meter shot.
Five friends.
Four quarters.
Three cheers.
Two breaths.
One survivor.

CHAPTER TWENTY-THREE

8:15 A.M.

I'M CARSICK. BRAIN DIZZY. STOMACH TWISTY.
Like I'm driving way up into the mountains. Or higher, then higher. Up and up. My head goes so light it floats.

My toes and fingers float, too.

There's no ground beneath me.

It's water.

I think I see Charlie. Reaching out to me. I spread my fingers. Want his hand. But he's too far away. I can't grasp it.

"Let go, Ruby Tuesday," he says.

I'm a limp body along the cold surface of the swimming pool.

The drain gulps beneath me.

Glug, glug, glug.

It pulls me toward it.

My stomach buckles first. I fold in half like a piece of paper.

Down, down, down I go.
Until I am pulled all the way under.
I am floppy arms and mermaid hair.
I am weak bones and popping bubbles.
I am here and I am not.
It feels good to let go.
It's a relief to disappear into the drain.

CHAPTER TWENTY-FOUR

11:01 A.M.

SOMETHING CRUNCHES. MOVES. PANTS. SNIFFS.
Someone is here. *Something* is here.

It presses against my hand. My eyelids flutter. I make out the black damp nose of a dog. It pulls back. Barks. Barks again.

Footsteps pound. Slip on uneven ground.

Thump, thump, slide.

Shouts. Whistles. Echoes. People.

And then it comes.

Fingertips to my pulse. A voice. A man. A stranger. Help at last.

"Right here! I've got someone!"

The fingertips wrap around mine. A full hand squeezes. The voice asks me to squeeze back. My hand is so small compared to this other one.

One day I will meet someone with bigger hands than mine.

Rough calluses and strong fingers. "*Squeeze,*" the voice says again.

It's effort. My fingers barely bend. I try to grip. Force the faintest movement. Then slip.

"Good, good," the voice says. "We're gonna get you out."

In my mind, I nod. Say thank you.

"Over here! Bring a board!" he calls to the others.

More footsteps. More people. The crackle of rocks slipping. The echoing thump of rubble being cleared away. Space opens up around me.

Hope.

I can't tell how many are here. Talking. Shouting. All of them in heavy boots. Stomping. Slipping. Crunching. They smell of sweat, acrid like onions. And their faces are smudged with too much dirt and soot to make out the details of them. How many others have they saved? How many hours have they worked?

Inch by inch, they prep me. It's meticulous.

It takes hours.

It takes years.

My neck is clamped into a brace. Hard and plastic. I can't move. But I'm finally lifted. Gently. Slowly. The shock of movement makes me shiver. Everything shakes. My stomach. My hands. My chest. My teeth.

I'm strapped to a board, hard and flat. But stable. The snaps of buckles echo. Straps across my shoulders. Down my chest. Around my legs. I know it's for my own good. To keep me safe.

But it feels like being stuck again, and part of me wants to fight against it.

Then a soft blanket. Clean. Comfort.

I'm lifted. Carefully. Slowly.

"Watch her arm." A woman now, her voice clear. Firm. In charge.

I twist. Trapped again.

On this board.

In these clamps.

But the world around me is real. It isn't dust and dirt and teetering table legs. It isn't the too-dark darkness. It isn't Charlie silenced. It is whole and wide-open and feels like it could go on forever. It's so much bigger than me.

I'm a smudge against the sky.

The one with the big hands still talks in my ear. Tells me I'm safe now.

"Charlie," I try to say. But my mouth is too dry.

I try to point. To tell them where he is. I don't want to leave my friend behind. Because they're taking me somewhere else. We jostle our way across, up and over and through. I swing to the side when someone slips against the crackle of rubble under their feet. They steady me quickly. Make me flat again.

The air smells different. Not like salt and ocean. It's charred. Burnt.

The big hand squeezes mine once more.

"Stay with me," the voice says. "Stay."

GAME CHANGER

Sometimes you're losing. Sometimes you think things are over, but they're not. Because sometimes there are comebacks.

You just have to hold on.

Like water polo finals and the fourth quarter of a tied game. The clock ticked down to one minute and twelve seconds underneath stadium lights and winter fog. The other team looked tired. Heavy arms and heavier legs dragged like fishing nets through the water.

I felt the heaviness, too, but I felt the want to win more.

I wrestled with a girl in front of the goal. Kicked. Scratched. Twisted. Around and around we went while the water kicked up. She pulled me under. The referee saw it and ejected her.

A new shot clock set.

We had a chance to win the game.

We had a chance to survive.

Coach called a time-out.

We swam to the wall.

Coach kneeled on the deck with his clipboard.

He drew lines and arrows and circles to map out the play.

We watched him draw and talk while we dragged Gatorade into our mouths from a sports bottle being passed around.

Coach was calm.

Coach was confident.

I knew where I was supposed to go.

Thea knew when to pass.

The others knew to push in.

Mila would guard the goal.

We took position.

The whistle blew.

In a blur we went.

I had to concentrate. No time to think. Just react.

The ball was in my hand and I pushed back with an elbow out. I felt others moving in closer to me. I was going to have two girls on me soon.

I watched the net.

The goalie eggbeatered until she rose out of the water. She pivoted from the waist up, her arms spread wide like airplane wings.

She leaned left, so I shot right.

The ball went in, swishing against the net, and lodging itself into the corner.

The stands went wild. Parents shook pom-poms. The boys' water polo team jumped up and down, pumping their fists in the air and stomping their feet against the metal bleachers until the sound echoed through the stadium.

Boom-boom. Boom-boom. Boom-boom.

The goalie sank underwater in frustration. Bubbles bubbled. She came back up and slapped the surface of the water. It bounced off her hand and into the air.

The scoreboard ticked up a point on our side. It was 6–5. But the game wasn't over yet. We had to hold them. We had to hang on.

The ref blew her whistle.

The other team pressed in with the ball. I pushed forward, raised a hand in the air to block the shot.

"No foul, no foul!" Coach shouted from the bench.

A girl on the other team twisted.

She saw her chance. She swooped. She turned. She shot. And suddenly the ball was heading for our goal.

The players on the bench drew in a collective breath.

Mila launched herself from the water. Spread her arm wide to the right. The ball smacked off her palm, blocking the shot. She wrestled for it. Took possession.

The cheers from the crowd got louder, making the air electric.

Mila passed me the ball. I took control, swimming off in the other direction, toward the other side of the pool, toward the other goal.

The lights of the scoreboard blazed. The shot clock ticked down.

My team spread out in a wide circle in the water. Juliette passed. I passed. Iris passed. Thea passed. Running down the clock as everyone in the stands counted down.

Ten.

And the rest of the team on the bench.

Nine. Eight. Seven.

And my mom.

Six. Five. Four.

And then us.

Three. Two.

One.

The buzzer went off and the water swelled up like the ocean. We were a mass of kicking and screaming and elation in the middle of the pool. Two players on the deck pushed Coach into the water, clothes and all. And then everyone else jumped in. And we were a celebration. Someone from the local newspaper took a photo. Parents snapped pictures from the stands. In the air, the announcement on the loudspeaker said we won.

We won.

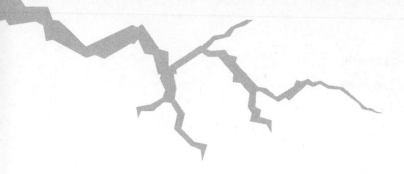

CHAPTER TWENTY-FIVE

11:38 A.M.

THE BIG HANDS AND THE CALM VOICE ARE still here. "What's your name?" He speaks strong and clear. Like I can trust him. I can tell him.

"Ru—by," I manage. It's weak. Garbled. Like Charlie's last breath.

"Ruby?" He squeezes my hand. "We're gonna take care of you, Ruby."

All the people are here to help.

Charlie isn't here.

My mom isn't. I need her. Where is she?

We are going and going. People are talking and talking. They talk to me and I try to answer, but the world is so fuzzy. I just want to sleep. Everyone around me talks to one another. Saying numbers. Naming places.

There's a rush. Moving. Pushing. Fast.

I squint my eyes open. There are so many people. There are tents. Like the drill at school. One tent is filled with people covered all the way up with white sheets. Even over their faces. I can't see them. They don't move.

I can't move.

What if I'm like them? What if this is what it feels like to be dead?

I try to move so I'll know I'm not the same. I'm too stiff. Stuck. But then I remember the neck brace. The straps around me. All of it holding me in. Too tight. No space. Like the rubble. I can't breathe.

I'm still trapped.

I want to scream.

I want to bust through.

"It's okay," the man with the big hands and the calm voice says when I shake. My hand is still in his. "We're taking you to the triage tents, where the doctors can help you. I'm gonna stay with you until we get there, okay, Ruby?"

I try to nod. The brace won't let me.

We push past empty space. Black asphalt. Ambulance vans and bright red fire trucks. My gaze scrapes across the sides of them. Shiny. Slick.

We go into another tent. It's not people covered in sheets here. There's pain. Screams. Howls. I want to cover my ears but I can't move my arms.

I want to move.

I want to talk.

I want to leave.

Someone shouts above me. A woman. "Respiration's under thirty. Cap refill is not immediate. Cannot follow simple commands. Possible sepsis. Tagged *immediate*."

They're talking about me.

I'm immediate. I'm a label, not a person.

I want to know what's happening

I want to know somebody and I want somebody to know me.

I close my eyes. Drifting.

The calm voice is in my ear one more time. An electric jolt. His big hand squeezes mine. "You've got this. Stay with us." I try my hardest to squeeze back. I try with everything I have. I manage something just barely. "That's my girl."

The lip of a bottle hits my mouth. Water. I gulp. Sputter.

"Slow," someone says.

I drink again. Slower.

A shout from outside the tent. "Multiples at Shore and Sunset. We need everyone."

The big hand lets go of mine. Pushes back.

I try to say *Don't leave*. It's a whisper.

"I have to go," he says. "This is the part where I let the doctors step in and I go help someone else. Another person like you."

I want to cry because I don't want to be alone again.

He swipes his hand across my forehead. "You need someone else now. My job was to get you here."

And then I'm being lifted up again. One person and another

one are doing it. What's happening? Where am I now? They set me down on a cot so the big hands and the calm voice can take the stretcher. Someone scribbles on something, and I watch as they set it down on top of my chest.

A red tag.

I'm poked. Prodded. A clear mask goes over my nose and mouth. So much fresh, clean air. Not dusty like the rubble. Not singed and burnt like the sky. I can breathe. Something stings inside my arm. I feel it moving up and up through my veins.

The pain fades. I'm fuzzy. My thoughts fizzle.

I'm dandelion fluff.

I'm a floating balloon.

I can't keep my eyes open. They're so heavy. I can't hang on. I'm breaking my promise to the big hands and the calm voice. And my mom. And Charlie.

But I'm too tired to stay.

CHAPTER TWENTY-SIX

12:00 P.M.

MOVING AGAIN. OUT AND THROUGH THE
tent. And then I'm slid into the back of an ambulance. Metal
against metal. I want to protest.

I just got out, don't put me back in.

I try to speak. "Where?" My voice garbled. Not clear. Not
strong. My head so fuzzy from that stuff in my arm.

"I have one immediate going to University Med." The man
who pushed me here. And then the numbers again. Something
over something. Sepsis. More things I don't understand. "Go, go!"

Chaotic. Quick. They're in a hurry to save me. I feel it in
the shuffle.

Above me is the wail of the siren.

Below me is the push of movement.

I'm going away. Farther and farther.

I'm fading.

CHAPTER TWENTY-SEVEN

12:30 P.M.

I COME TO WHEN WE MOVE AGAIN. TWO PEO-
ple pushing me. One at my head. One at my feet. There's rattling underneath me, the squeal of metal wheels. My heart races too fast with memories. Rubble. Rescue. Big hands. Calm voice. My vision blurs but I don't miss the shiny building. The big hospital sign. No! I hate hospitals. Hospitals are where people go to die.

I wiggle. Try to move. To break free. But a hand on my shoulder steadies me. Then I'm through the doors. Across the floors.

Pushed. Pushed. Pushed.

Shouts.

Turn. Turn. My body sways from one side to the other, the straps holding me in, keeping me from falling as we turn again. Through hallways. Around corners.

Until we jerk to a sudden stop.

"Here?" someone says.

"Five flights," the other answers.

I try to focus on which voice is which.

Then my stretcher is compact. The wheels fold underneath me and I'm carried instead of rolled. We're going up. Stairs. A turn. More stairs. My head is heavy with exhaustion and fuzz. But still I see the horror. There are bodies. *Bodies.* Covered in sheets on the landings. Piled up. One and then another on top of that. Just like I thought. Just like I knew hospitals would be.

And then the rotting-meat smell of decay. Creeping. Crawling up my nostrils. Making me choke.

I squirm, the straps digging into my shoulders and thighs, my heart stuttering with the fear they'll leave me here. But then the one at my feet heaves the stairwell door open. We all snap back when the heavy door stops short against something on the inside. I grip the sides of my stretcher, fearing I'll fall off. Get lost in the pile of bodies. Dead and forgotten.

Bang, bang. A fist against the wall by the door.

"Here!" the man at my feet shouts.

Footsteps shuffle. The door creaks open more. They're forcing me in. The one at my head stays. The one at my feet goes.

"I've got her." A woman now. All-white coat with a clipboard and a pencil. Tracking arrivals.

A snapping sound, and I'm transferred from one cot to another. The wheels on the new cot slip out from underneath me and the woman in the white coat kicks something, a brake, that makes it stop. Frozen. The straps fall loose. I can move again, but I'm too tired to do it. I feel sweaty and sick.

"Name?" she says.

"Ruby." The syllables scratch against my throat.

"What's that?" the woman says.

"Ruby." One of the guys from the ambulance. "She's in and out. Puncture wound to her left arm. Possible sepsis."

I open my eyes to him, wanting to see this person who knows so much about me when I know nothing about him. I catch the scruff on his face. The dark circles under his eyes. The tired slope of his shoulders. The stains on his coat. Dirt. Blood.

He's been doing this for days.

"Last name? Age?" The woman again. Straight, shiny hair. A mole under the corner of her eye. Tiny gold hoops in her ears.

He shakes his head. "Wish I knew."

I try to say *Seventeen,* but I slur. Unclear. Only the *S* sound comes out. A long hiss. I try again because I want to give them something. Answer the questions he can't. But my whole age stays stuck on my tongue.

I lie there hissing, "Sssssss."

"We've got it from here," the woman says. Is she talking to me or the man who brought me here? The one with the face scruff and the tired shoulders.

He nods. Turns to go. I tug at the edge of his jacket to stop him. I want to know his name. To thank him.

"Thhhhh—" I manage.

He looks at my face. I focus my eyes on his. Hoping that's enough for him to understand how grateful I am.

He smiles. Gentle. "I know."

"Good luck out there," the woman says to his back as he leaves.

She moves my leg, bending it at the knee. She moves my left arm to rest it across my stomach. I'm clay and she's molding me. I let her. I don't resist because I can't. I can only squint at the lights above me. They aren't bright and fluorescent. They're soft. Flickering. Barely there. Like me. Running on fumes.

Someone else bangs through the stairwell door, calling for help. The woman stops moving me to take off with her clipboard and her pencil.

Around me, the hallway echoes with the sounds of labored breathing. Grunts. Groans. Like Charlie.

I want to be somewhere else.

I struggle to lift my head. To see. To know. Where else can I go?

But there's only an endless sea of people. They surround me. On cots in front of me. And next to me. If there's space, there's a person. Every hallway. Every door. Every room. Every square inch has people in it. I reach out. I want to be able to touch them the same way I wanted to touch Charlie. To know we're all in this together. I couldn't reach Charlie, but maybe I can reach them. I stretch my fingers to connect. I catch the soft edge of the shirt of someone next to me.

We're all here. Crammed in side by side. Cot-to-cot.

Hope-to-hope.

CHAPTER TWENTY-EIGHT

4:03 P.M.

MY WORLD WHIRS. I GO OUT. I GO IN. VISION blurry. Brain hazy.

I try to move, but it feels like swimming. Like I'm trying to grip the lip of the pool gutter but never getting there, my fingertips slipping down the edge whenever I grab for it.

I struggle to focus. I'm in a new room. A room within a room. I'm covered in gauze and tender bruises and crisp clean sheets. There's a clear plastic bag with clear liquid inside. It's hanging from a hook on a portable metal stand next to me. I follow the tube from the bag to my hand.

Am I like my dad? Am I waiting to die?

There aren't any windows, and the air is blue-gray from dimmed lights. A chair sits in the corner with my dirty sweatshirt on it. Charlie's journal on top. A reminder of who I am and where

I came from and who I know. The life I have outside of here. The life I had before. My eyes scrape across the sliding glass doors of my room and focus on the workstation outside. It sits in the middle and the doors to other hospital rooms make an octagon around it. The workstation reminds me of a spaceship; a futuristic-looking pod full of desks and computers where the doctors and nurses can monitor patients. And in the center of all that is the static of a voice on a radio sounding newsy and informative, relaying only the most important information. The sliding glass doors of other rooms are spread out like an octagon around the workstation. I can see into the one across from mine. There's a woman in a chair. She wears a yellow shirt as bright as the sun.

She holds the hand of someone in the bed.

Wait.

Charlie?

Did the big hands and the calm voice get him out, too?

My body wakes with hope. A rush of warmth to my insides. I try to sit up. I want to stand. I want to go to him. I want to hear him call me Ruby Tuesday.

But all too quickly the sinking crush of truth comes.

Charlie isn't here. Charlie is dead. I held his hand. I know.

His words are in a journal on top of my sweatshirt.

I deflate with the pain of it.

Why him and not me?

I want to shout it. I want to know where I am. I want to change positions but this bed is too small. The sheets are too tight. I kick my feet to loosen them.

I roll to the side.

The tube to my arm pinches. Hurts.

I hiss.

Next to me, something beeps. I look up. I'm a summary of jagged lines and numbers on a screen.

A nurse in pale pink scrubs rushes in. Her hair is pulled into a bun that sits slumped on top of her head. I squint. Make out the blurry name tag on her shirt. *Cathy.*

"You're awake," she says, smiling. Gentle. Calm. Reassuring.

"I—"

She checks the monitor. Rights me to my back. Tucks in my sheet. Too tight again. I kick it free as soon as she finishes, all of it so much effort. She takes note. Lets it be. When she reaches up to adjust the plastic bag of clear liquid, I notice a faded black T-shirt hanging out of the bottom of her scratchy scrubs. I want it to be a concert tee. I want to ask her about which band it is and when she saw them. Are they her favorite? Did she sing along to all their songs? The shirt brushes my arm. So soft. Like a baby blanket. It's a comfort against my raw skin, making me miss my mom and my own bed.

My mom.

I look for her. In this room. In this blue-gray light. I want to reach out and touch her. See her sitting in a chair, waiting for me, like that woman across the pod in the bright yellow shirt. Keeping watch. Radiating like sunlight.

But there is only emptiness.

Where is she?

"Mom." My voice is raspy. Indecipherable.

"Let's see if this helps."

Nurse Cathy untwists the safety seal from a small bottled water in her pocket. She reaches over to fill a blue plastic cup on a nearby table. She sticks a straw in the cup. Helps me sit. Holds the straw to my lips.

I suck. Swallow. But my throat is swollen. Raw. I wince. Nurse Cathy pulls the cup away.

"Okay?" she asks.

I nod. Push my open face toward the cup. I want more. I smack my lips. A baby bird in the nest. She holds the straw to my mouth. I suck again. It doesn't hurt as bad to swallow this time. It coats my dry throat. It makes me think I can form words. The water isn't enough.

"Food?"

"You're getting there. IV for now. No solids yet."

When the small cup is drained, I manage another word. "Mom?"

Nurse Cathy squeezes my shoulder. Shakes her head. My eyes pool. Wet. Glassy. And Nurse Cathy goes swirly in my vision.

I need to ask more, but then the next thought comes swooping in.

"Charlie?"

Nurse Cathy's eyebrows crease in the middle, the barely-there wrinkle transforms into a deep crevice. "Is your name Charlie?"

Does she not know who I am? Does she not know my name is Ruby? I thought the woman in the white coat wrote it down.

Nobody here knows anything about me. And if I'm not awake to tell them, they'll never know. I could end up being just another someone piled in the stairwell landing. Or like Charlie in the laundromat. If someone finds him, how will they know who he is? I need to tell someone where to find him. To name him.

I shake my head. Try again to say what I mean. "Charlie."

She flicks her gaze to me. "We have John Does. Jane Does. I haven't met a Charlie, but that doesn't mean they're not here."

That's not what I mean. I know he isn't here. He's in the laundromat. Gone. I want someone to get him. To bring him home.

I sink back into the pillows.

I am a lump. I am a bruise. I am a broken heart. I am alone.

"You need to rest," Nurse Cathy says, pushing a syringe of clear liquid into the port attached to my hand. I feel the warmth of it go up my arm. A sudden flash of heat like when I peed in the rubble. The warmth stays this time. The pain falls away.

"Where is . . . my . . . mom?" The words stumble out. Wobbly. Halfway there. "Is . . . she . . . at work? Is . . . she . . . here?"

"I don't know. People are everywhere." Nurse Cathy's voice drifts, like the beginning of a bedtime story. The medicine in my veins reaches my brain, and I see people floating around in the air, above the earth, arms and legs splayed, like slow-motion jumpers on a trampoline.

I reach my hand out to catch them but only my fingers flutter.

People are everywhere. Don't you see them floating by?

DAY FOUR

MONDAY

DAY FIVE

TUESDAY

DAY SIX

WEDNESDAY

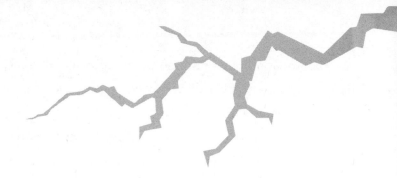

CHAPTER TWENTY-NINE

7:10 P.M.

I JOLT AWAKE. SIT UP STRAIGHT. I'M NOT floating anymore. My eyes fly around the room, darting to sliding glass doors and empty corners. My sweatshirt. Charlie's journal. The empty chair in my room. The woman in yellow in the room across from mine. She's waiting like my mom would. Like she must be. Where is my mom now? She must've stepped out for only a minute. She must be tired from sitting at my bedside. But surely the relief of finding me would make up for the exhaustion. Right? She wouldn't leave me once she'd found me. She'd be like the woman in the yellow shirt.

"Mom?" I say. "Mom!" Louder. My voice is clear again. Strong enough to shout. The woman in yellow turns her head to look at me. Is she a mom? Does she recognize my need?

The lines on my monitor go up and down and it beeps as my heart races faster. What do the beeps mean? Do they mean I'm dying? Is everyone just waiting?

The nurse rushes in. Her name tag. *Cathy*. I remember her. She has new scrubs. These ones are blue. A pale green T-shirt underneath. I imagine another band. Another concert. This one all girls with pounding bass lines and screeching guitars.

"Where's my mom?"

Nurse Cathy's face falls.

"Honey." She crosses to my bed. Scrunches her eyes. "Sweetie. I told you. The other day . . ."

The other day? What did she tell me the other day? I remember her shirt. Her name. The water. The fizzy feeling up my arm. I don't remember days. I don't remember my mom.

"Is she here?"

"We're trying to find her."

Everything slides out from under me. Like the legs of my bed have collapsed. Like the walls of the laundromat. It all folds in.

Memories. Hope. Want. Dread.

My mom. Charlie. Leo. My friends. All that I've lost and still might lose. "Have you checked her office? Have you checked our house?" I know it isn't Nurse Cathy's job, but it makes me angry she isn't combing the streets looking for my mom the way I would if I could.

And then.

"Do you even know who she is? How do you know who I am?"

Nurse Cathy points to my sweatshirt. I see it for what it is now. Filthy. Torn. Beat-up. Bloody. A reminder of everything that happened in the rubble.

"We know your name is Ruby. Ruby who plays water polo for Pacific Shore High according to the big logo on the back of your sweatshirt. We've been waiting for you to fill in the rest."

"I'm Ruby Babcock. I need to get out of here." My eyes dart to my monitor. To the tube running from my hand to the clear bag of clear liquid. To the workstation filled with doctors and nurses. To the room on the other side. "I hate hospitals."

Hospitals are where people go to die.

"I get it."

"I have to find my mom."

"Ruby, honey, we want to help you find her. But taking care of you comes first. And with communication down—"

"No."

I sit up straight, pull my legs over the side of the bed, and stand up. Determined. That's it. It's up to me. Just like I had to get out of the rubble. Now I have to get out of the hospital. I have to get to my house. See if it's still standing. Or I have to go to my mom's office. Maybe she's trapped under her desk the same way I had been trapped at the laundromat. Maybe she's run out of water. Maybe she's broken. Or maybe she's in this very same hospital. I can go room-to-room. Pound on doors. Shout her name.

I step forward and my legs buckle like someone kicked me behind the knees, falling out from under me as I crumble to the floor. I push myself back up. Sway.

And then the thought I don't want.

What if my mom is like Charlie? Buried. Anonymous. What if she's under a sheet in a stairwell, piled up among strangers?

I hold my hands to my stomach. Try to keep the emotion in so I don't break in the middle of this room.

Nurse Cathy tries to coax me back to the bed with a firm grip around my waist, but I twist and manage to wiggle free. I remember how strong I am in the water and summon it now. Nurse Cathy and I are wrestling in front of the goal and I need to make the shot. It's good that I'm so much taller than she is. It gives me an advantage.

"I see you haven't lost your athletic skills." She grabs for but misses the back of my gown.

I push forward, pulling the pole with the metal hook holding the clear bag of clear liquid with me. The wheels scrape. Wobble unsteadily, like my knees. I stand at the opening of the sliding glass doors, but I don't know where to go. The handful of people sitting in the workstation look up from their computer monitors and their coffee cups and the static radio. That woman's yellow shirt lights up the room behind them. I want someone to care about me the way she cares about whoever is in that bed.

Nurse Cathy wraps a strong arm around my waist. Steadies the metal stand. "While it's great to see you on your feet, you're not ready. Back to bed with you."

"No." I untangle myself from her grasp. Push forward again. I'm wrestling in front of the goal in a water polo game, ready to shoot. But this place is blurring. Fizzy. Someone else is here. A woman wearing a lab coat with a stethoscope around her neck. She's a flash of motion. Like the woman at the laundromat who flipped the safety switches. Her arms reach out. She's the last thing I remember before I fall into darkness.

Gone.

CHAPTER THIRTY

7:30 P.M.

When I come to, I'm back in bed. Nurse Cathy stands on one side of me, fussing with my IV. The woman with the stethoscope is on the other side, leaning over me, pushing something that smells too minty-strong against my nose. I flick it away like a buzzing bug. A nuisance.

"Ruby," Nurse Cathy says, "this is Doctor Patel. I get that you're ready to bust out of here, but you need to listen to what she has to say."

Doctor Patel takes a breath. "It's very important that you stay in bed." She looks at me. Wants her concern to sink in. But my concern is elsewhere. Its focus is someplace beyond this room.

"I have to find my mom." I look at Nurse Cathy for help. She heard me. She knows how important this is.

"I understand. But you've been through a lot," Doctor Patel

says. "You were dehydrated and unconscious when you arrived three days ago."

"Three days?"

She nods. "You came in with something called a staph infection; do you know what that is?"

"No."

"It's serious. It can lead to sepsis. When you arrived, your blood pressure was too low. Your heartbeat was erratic. And you were running a high fever. We've been treating you with an antibiotic called vancomycin because the cut on your arm needed stitches and the infection was resistant to penicillin. Your rescuers got you here just in time."

I remember the jagged overhang in my safe space. The reach for my phone. My arm slicing open like cake when I pushed too hard to grab it. The way my pain had a heartbeat. The way my arm felt like it was on fire for the hours that sunk into days. The fire is dull now. From medicine, I guess.

"You're a lucky one," Nurse Cathy says.

"Am I?"

Doctor Patel smiles. "You are. But you still need to take it easy so you can heal completely. We were giving you medicine to help you sleep. You don't seem like you need it anymore. But I do need you to stay in bed." Her eyes are gentler than I'd realized. They match her voice. "You need close monitoring and lots of rest. Can you let us do our part while you do yours?"

Nurse Cathy nods. "Listen to Doc Patel, sweetie."

"Why?"

"She knows what's best. We've worked shifts together for a decade. She's one of our top doctors and I trust her. You should, too." She leans in. "And if you want in on a little secret, she's also a movie genius. She sweeps our ICU Oscar pool every year."

How can Nurse Cathy be talking about movies? How can she be so calm? When I'm sitting here worrying about whether or not I'll ever see my mom again?

"Look," Doctor Patel says firmly, so opposite of Nurse Cathy's *sweetie* and *honey* and pats on the shoulder. "You've lived through a catastrophic 7.8-magnitude earthquake, Ruby. The Big One. There are repercussions from the ocean to the desert. Water supplies are limited. There are casualties in the thousands. This hospital is being run on generators. Phones aren't working. The internet isn't working. No TV, so we can't even fully keep track of the news as it breaks. Reuniting family members has been a difficult and arduous task, not just here but everywhere."

"But my mom—"

Nurse Cathy nods. Tries to soothe me with a look. "We know."

My questions pile on top of one another like the rubble. How can anyone think I'd even want to be alive in a world without my mom in it? The hours in a world without Charlie in it have been bad enough, and I just met him. And what about everyone else? All the people I care about. Leo. Thea. Iris. Juliette. My teammates. Coach. And yes, Mila. Where are they? If everyone's gone, what would be the point of my going on?

Doctor Patel says, "Teams of people are working hard to

reconnect family members. And it is happening. But it's taking a lot of time with so many systems down. We want to find your mom, too. And when we do, you will be the first to know. I promise."

I fist my hands in frustration. "You can't really promise that."

"I can do my best." Doctor Patel doesn't look at me.

Neither does Nurse Cathy.

Because they know I'm right. They might never find her. And if they do, she might not be alive.

Nurse Cathy says, "There are FEMA crews out there. And the American Red Cross. They've set up shelters all over. And there are everyday people crossing state lines to pitch in. So many folks are out there trying to help."

I nod. That's great, but I can't see how it helps me.

I'm so hungry. The realization sinks me.

"Food?" I ask.

"Certainly." Doctor Patel looks at Nurse Cathy. "I think she's ready for something besides liquids. Jell-O maybe? Do we have any left?"

"On it," Nurse Cathy says, and heads out the sliding glass door.

Doctor Patel stays with me. "The earthquake has been devastating. We need more people like you out there. To help with cleanup and getting us back to normal. I have a feeling you can do a lot of good when you get out of here. So will you rest up and get strong, Ruby?"

"Okay."

"Good."

Doctor Patel leaves, and Nurse Cathy returns with a snack pack–size Jell-O cup like the ones my mom used to put in my school lunches in elementary school.

"I got you the last one."

She sets it on a tray in front of me, peels the lid off. I spoon a wobbly bite into my mouth and feel it go down my throat all smooth and easy. I hum with relief, my tongue wrapping around the sweet taste of it. I spoon another bite. Swallow.

"My mom used to pack Jell-O in my school lunches," I mumble through a mouthful.

"Mine too." Nurse Cathy smiles. "Strawberry is the best flavor, don't you think?"

"Right now, it's pretty much the most delicious thing I've ever eaten."

"My mom used to buy the variety pack, and my sister and I would argue over who got the strawberry ones."

I take another bite. "Who won?"

"My sister. Usually." She studies me. "You remind me of her."

"Why? Because I keep arguing with you?"

Nurse Cathy laughs. A real laugh. Like Charlie in the rubble. It's amazing how joy can be found in such horrifying places. And that kindness can happen with the simplest of gestures. Like a cup of Jell-O.

"For the record, you remind me of my sister because you don't give up. You're a fighter just like she is."

"I don't feel like a fighter."

"You are. Fighting is what got you here."

But I know it's not just me. It's people, too. From Charlie to Cathy. From the big hands and the calm voice to Doctor Patel. From the woman who flipped the safety switches to the woman in the hallway with the clipboard. So many people have fought to get me here. They believed in my strength.

I have to believe in it, too.

BELIEVE

Leo had rules and curfews and two parents who had been high school sweethearts. There were weekly Sunday dinners with his grandparents and Dave & Buster's birthday parties for his little brother. His whole family attended every swim meet, and his mom was a dedicated member of the PTA and the aquatics booster club.

I could only imagine what he thought when he came to my house and my mom had left a fluorescent pink Post-it on the fridge to tell me she was working late and I was on my own for dinner.

"Should we DoorDash?" I asked Leo, pulling my phone from my back pocket and tapping on the app.

"We can do whatever." He made his way to my living room, flopped down on the couch, and aimed the remote control at the TV to turn it on. "I don't hate this, though."

"What do you mean?" I abandoned my phone on the counter and flopped down beside him.

"Watching TV. Not even thinking about dinner." He lingered on a channel that aired only black-and-white television shows from the fifties. My mom watched it sometimes, too. "It's kind of nice to walk into a house and not have my mom breathing down my neck with a million questions about my AP chem test and my swim times." He leaned his head against the back cushions of the couch. "I feel like I can breathe." And then he did. He let out a long exhale and his whole body seemed to decompress, melting into the cushions. "I don't even have to set the table for dinner."

I thought about coming home alone. My own breath sometimes stopped until I was inside and had flicked on the lights, making the dark bright. Safer. Warmer.

"Right," I said.

And it's not like my mom wasn't around. She came to my games. We sometimes did stuff on the weekends. On most nights she was home for dinner. But since there were only two of us, it was quiet even when we were both there.

Part of me envied the noise and organized chaos at Leo's house. The juggling of sports schedules and the chore list tacked to the inside of the pantry door.

Is it true that we always want what we don't have?

Did I want a sibling and a dad?

I couldn't say.

But *maybe*.

I hadn't thought about it until that moment when Leo seemed to think something about my life was better than his.

Even though it was probably just the peace and quiet and room to breathe.

I flung my leg over Leo's knee, and we sat there on the couch, flipping through channels, eventually getting sucked into whatever reality show was on MTV.

We didn't order dinner.

Because we both fell asleep.

Grueling workout schedules caught up to both of us, and we were like an old married couple that couldn't stay up past ten o'clock on a Friday night. We both jolted awake when my mom came home, the kitchen door clicking shut too loudly behind her as she came into the house from the garage.

She wandered into the living room and said hello to both of us.

I discreetly swiped at my mouth, worried I'd drooled all over Leo's shoulder as I had a tendency to do when I was the kind of bone-tired that made me pass out on the couch.

All clear.

I studied my mom as she checked the dead bolt on the front door.

She wasn't in work clothes. She was in a little black dress with spaghetti straps. And spiky heels with thin straps of ribbon that crisscrossed her ankles. She smiled to herself, like she'd suddenly remembered a funny story someone had told her. I could smell her perfume from where I was sitting. And something else I couldn't put my finger on. Liquor? Cigarette smoke? Her hair was mussed, too, like she'd been driving around in a convertible with the top down.

"You worked late?" I asked cautiously.

"Huh?" She balanced on one leg as she unbuckled the strap of a high heel. "Yes, right. Busy day." She cleared her throat. "Long day." She unbuckled her other heel and dangled both her shoes from her fingertips. "Well, I'm going to shower."

"'Night," I said.

"Good night, you two," my mom said as she headed up the stairs.

I watched her as she went, mumbling into Leo's shoulder, "I don't believe her."

"About what?"

"She wasn't at work."

He shrugged. "Where else would she have been?"

"I don't know. But I don't believe her."

"You have to believe her. She's your mom."

CHAPTER THIRTY-ONE

8:30 P.M.

I NEED A PHONE. I NEED TO MAKE CALLS.

First to my mom, then to Leo.

I need to find my people.

"I want to call my mom."

"The phones aren't working. I know it's frustrating, but—"

"I want to try."

"Okay, Ruby." Nurse Cathy goes to the workstation. Comes back. Hands me a cordless phone. She leaves again to give me privacy. I dial. And wait.

When I dial my mom, nothing happens. Not a busy signal. Not a ring. Nothing. I call our landline next. It rings and rings and rings. But it's an old-timey ring that doesn't sound normal. Like it isn't real. I imagine that ring echoing through our empty house. I don't get sent to voicemail, either. Proof it's not working.

I redial her cell. Then home. I am a ping-pong ball going back and forth. Cell. Home. Cell. Home. My fingers shake, slip. I punch the numbers wrong and have to start over again. I grip the phone harder, willing my mom to answer.

Cathy pokes her head in. "Anything?"

"Not yet." Every unanswered ring is a punch to my gut. I can't look at Nurse Cathy. I can't look through the sliding glass doors. Or at the woman in the yellow shirt. I can't look at any of the things I've been looking at since I woke up here. I can only focus on the pile of white sheets covering my legs. I grab a handful of the soft cotton and squeeze. I channel all my frustration into that bunched-up heap in my hand while my other hand grips the phone.

Our home phone rings endlessly.

I let it keep going.

I rock. Back and forth. The sheets move with me.

I want some part of my old life to answer. To pick up. To be alive.

To be okay.

Nurse Cathy watches me rock. "Is there someone else, maybe?" There's an underlying note of worry in her tone. The way Charlie sounded when he got nervous in the rubble.

I *should* try to call someone else, but I don't know any numbers from my contacts list. Who does? I'd seen Leo's name light up my screen thousands of times in the last seven months, but it didn't show his number. And the landline numbers of any of my friends? No way. How did I not pay attention to any of this stuff before?

I want to call Coach, but I don't know his number by heart, either.

I remember being told during an earthquake drill at school that family members should all check in with a designated family member living out of state. I'm sure my mom would call her mom, but I don't know my grandma's phone number in Seattle any better than I know Leo's.

I want to pull my hair. I'm so mad at myself for not knowing anything that can help me.

Emergency plans assume something. They assume you're in a place where you have access to everything you need. Food. Water. Phone numbers. A change of clothes. Your mom. Your house. They assume family members are all together. That the car has a full tank of gas. That you have a pocketful of cash. That you have tampons and a toothbrush. They assume you have a plan.

Or maybe it's me who assumed.

I rack my brain for something else to do or someone else to call.

I actually do know Mila's number by heart because I've known her since before we were allowed to have cell phones. I've called Mila's house a million times.

I don't care if the only words she's said to me since New Year's Eve have been mean ones.

I dial her and wait. It rings and rings with that same old-timey sound our landline had. I hang up. Try again. Repeat. What if Mila isn't okay? What if we don't get a chance to talk again?

Stop. I can't go there.

"A lot of folks couldn't get back into their homes," Nurse Cathy says. "Too much damage. It's hard to know exactly where everyone is. Shelters. The street."

My insides bubble. I'm frantic and helpless at the same time. A volcano ready to combust.

This is useless. I'm useless. I remember that moment in the rubble when Charlie said he was useless and I promised him he wasn't. But now I know how he felt. Now I get it.

I'm here because of luck.

And Charlie. My new friend helped keep me alive.

"Maybe you can try again later," Nurse Cathy says.

I want to yell at her even though it isn't her fault. I'm her patient. She doesn't want me to freak out because it's her job to help me get well. I understand all of this. But right now, all I want to do is throw this phone into the sliding glass doors hard enough to make them shatter. Maybe it will make the woman in the yellow shirt turn around. Maybe she'll see me. Maybe she'll comfort me since my own mom can't.

I sink back into the bed. Nurse Cathy refills my cup of water. Holds it out to me, lets me take it in my own hands this time. I suck down half of it without taking a breath.

"Is everything gone? Outside of here. Is it all gone?"

"It's bad." She winces. "Unrecognizable, even."

I regret asking.

"We're one of the few hospitals still up and running since we're farther away from the epicenter. The closer hospitals are too damaged to take patients. So the injured keep coming here. Like you." She shakes her head like she's had a hard time processing it all. "Days later and they keep finding people."

"Where were you when it happened?"

"Grocery store."

"Is your family okay?" Is she working at the hospital, helping other people, when her own family needs help? Are they missing, too?

"My people are all good. You're sweet to ask."

"Do you have kids?"

"I do. Twins. Kindergarten."

"What would you do if one of your kids was missing?"

She takes my water cup. "The same thing I'm sure *your* mom is doing: move mountains to find them."

"If she even can." It's the first time I've said the words out loud. I want to shove them back into my mouth and swallow them. What if saying them out loud could make them real? "I didn't mean that."

"I know." Nurse Cathy smiles at me. "How about this? How about you do what Doc Patel asked and work on getting better. So you have the strength to find your mom. To help. Cool?"

"I can do that."

"That makes me real happy to hear, Ruby. Your mom will be proud of you."

CHAPTER THIRTY-TWO

8:58 P.M.

I TOLD NURSE CATHY AND DOCTOR PATEL I'd stay in bed. To get strong. Get better. I still hate hospitals, but I realize the reason I'm alive is because of this place. And these people.

I wish Charlie had gotten this chance.

In the rubble he told me we'd get out and find a nice hospital where people would fix us up. I didn't want to go. He's the one who deserves to be here.

He deserves to have a better story.

I know the way his family will have to push through the murky waters of healing. Feeling guilty about the things they'd said or the things they wish they would've said. I want to meet them. Say how brave he was. How hard he fought to live.

I want to live.

Really live.

The way my mom says my dad did.

I want to shove aside all the petty things that were weighing me down when I walked into the laundromat last Friday. I want my mom to be happy. I want her to be happy with Coach. It doesn't matter if it's weird or if Mila makes fun of me. None of that matters anymore. Because I've spent the last six days fighting to stay alive.

That's way bigger than anything else. The most important thing in this world, the only one that matters, is being with the people you love.

Like the woman in the yellow shirt across the pod. She's here because the person in that bed is important to her. Every person in this hospital is another person's person. All of them going in and out, visiting other people in other rooms with their hands and faces clenched tight with worry. Covered in dust and blood and stitches.

I have to find my mom. It repeats like a mantra.

I imagine getting up out of this bed, pulling the tubes out of my arms, and pushing through the sliding glass doors of my room.

I won't falter this time.

I'll stay coherent.

I won't slip into the dark.

I will wave goodbye to the pod people in their spaceship workstation and walk away. They'll wish me luck because I will be confident in my leaving. I will pull on my sweatshirt and feel like myself again. Familiar. Comfortable. I don't care if it's dirty. I won't even care if my hospital gown pops open behind me. I will push forward down the hallway, moving toward the stairwell door, with Charlie's journal in my arms. Down I'll go to the front doors of the hospital. I will exit through them and drag cool air into my lungs. I will breathe in the fresh, bright smell of the big, wide world. I will search every inch of that big, wide world until I find my mom.

I will find her.

She will be okay.

I am her daughter. I need her. She needs me. We'll be reunited. And then we'll go home and live our life.

Coach Sanchez can come, too.

If that's what's meant to be.

I will appreciate the sunshine and smaller mundane things. I will eat burritos. Swim in the ocean. Read good books. Travel. Hug Leo. Leave flowers on graves. Let my mom love Coach.

And I'll never stop paying attention to the big things. Telling people that I love them. Trying to help Mila. Fighting for what I believe in.

Because we're all just trying to survive. Day to day. Year by year. In big ways and small.

I will remember and honor Charlie. Live a life of truth. Let go of blame. I wish I could've known him. I wish he could've been a part of my life forever.

Nurse Cathy walks in as I'm swiping at my tears with my bedsheets.

She hurries to my side. "What's wrong, honey?"

"I'm thinking about my friend. Charlie." I knot the sheets in my hand like a tissue.

She sits on the edge of my bed. "Tell me about your friend."

ONCE UPON A TIME

Once upon a time Charlie came home to start over.

Once upon a time Charlie had laundry and I had a plan.

Once upon a time it was a Friday in February and my day was the same as always.

Once upon a time there was a shift and a shatter.

Once upon a time there was ducking and covering and holding on tight.

Once upon a time there wasn't enough air.

Once upon a time there was a fear so deep in my gut that I can't believe I survived it.

Once upon a time Charlie and I had to talk each other through the rubble. And the fear. And the devastation.

Once upon a time we were each other's distraction.

Once upon a time Charlie had stories to tell.

Once upon a time it gave me peace to listen.

Once upon a time Charlie had guilt to reconcile.

Once upon a time I made a new friend in the most unexpected way.

DAY SEVEN

THURSDAY

CHAPTER THIRTY-THREE

2:38 A.M.

EVERYONE HAS GONE TO SLEEP. BUT SLEEP IN a hospital isn't really sleeping. People come in to poke and prod throughout the night. I roll over when the night nurse arrives. I give her my arm and she straps the Velcro blood pressure cuff around it. It squeezes tight then loosens as it lets out a breath to deflate.

Earlier, when I sweated through my gown and my sheets, Nurse Cathy knew how to change my bed without my getting out of it. Like those magicians who can pull tablecloths away yet leave all the dishes and knives and forks and glasses in place.

When she covered me up again, she left the sheets loose at my feet. Squeezed my toes to let me know she remembered.

Right now, the night nurse tries to tuck them in again.

I kick them free. "No."

"Okay," she says with a hint of sarcasm. *Okaaaaaay*. She sounds like Mila.

I take a cup of water and two pills from her. Nod. Do whatever she needs so I can go back to sleep. And wake up strong.

I'm already shutting my eyes again, letting my head hit the pillow, when a beeping sound jolts us both. It blasts through the ICU and between the crack of my sliding glass doors. Is it me? Is it my monitors? Am I okay?

The nurse leaves the cup in my hand. Ditches the blood pressure cuff by my bed. She rushes from my room and scrambles through the workstation to the room across from mine. There are too many doctors and nurses in there. I don't see the woman with the yellow shirt as bright as the sun. Her chair is empty.

Someone hovers above the bed. Holds two paddles from a defibrillator. Calls out, "Clear." The body bounces on the bed.

The beeping doesn't stop.

They do it again.

I remember Charlie telling me about his friend at the frat party and the defibrillator that came too late.

Did he watch them do this? Did he see?

The woman in the yellow shirt comes rushing in from the hallway. She cuts through the workstation to get to the room faster.

She screams, "No!" and drops the cup she's holding onto the floor. *Splat.*

She presses her hand to the sliding glass door and screams some more. She pounds on the glass.

She tries to shove her way into the room but a nurse pushes her back.

"Let them work," the nurse says.

"I was only gone for a minute."

That's how fast it happens.

One minute. Everything changes. Like Charlie. Like my dad.

Seconds tick by. On and on they go, while everyone tries to save whoever is in that room. I wish Charlie had gotten that chance. I hope this person can be saved since Charlie wasn't.

But then quiet settles in like fog. The beeping stops. The light flicks off. The darkness takes over. The doctors and nurses walk away. The woman in the yellow shirt crumbles into the arms of a nurse. She says no over and over and over again. I watch the nurse try to collect the pieces of the woman that are spilling out all over the floor.

I shut my eyes and instantly picture my mom in a random bed in a random room in a random hospital.

A midnight rush to save her life.

And then I picture her not there but somewhere worse. Someplace unknown.

I picture myself crumbling.

I push the thought away. I can't let it in.

I have to find her.

She has to find me.

"I'm sorry," I whisper to the woman in the yellow shirt outside the door of the room across from mine. It's not a prayer. It's an offering. To let her know I see her pain. I understand her pain. Even if I don't know her, I know her loss.

And the way she's breaking.

CHAPTER THIRTY-FOUR

9:00 A.M.

FOR BREAKFAST, I'M GIVEN LUKEWARM OAT-
meal that tastes like cardboard. I want real food. Something that
will sink into my stomach and stick to my insides. I want a cheese-
burger and french fries and a Coke from the Belmont Diner across
the street from school. But I bet the diner is gone.

Nurse Cathy, in another pair of soft pink scrubs, the hem
of a purple T-shirt peeking out, comes into my room while I'm
eating. The bun on top of her head droops lower today, as if
it's tired like her eyes. She looks like she's been working for a
week straight. It's possible. Probable. I take another bite of oat-
meal. It struggles down my throat before it sits like a rock in
my stomach.

"Good news." Nurse Cathy turns to me, hands on her hips.
"You've been cleared to get out of here today."

I shake my head. "I have nowhere to go." Is there still a home to go home to?

"Oh, sweetie, I'm sorry. Not the hospital. Just *here.* The ICU." She looks around my private space. "They've designated a special ward a couple floors up for kids like you."

"Like me?"

She pats my shoulder like she senses my distress. "Minors who still need medical attention and their parents."

"Parent."

"Our outreach team will meet with you and get all your information. They're working with FEMA to reconnect families. They've had tremendous success over the last few days."

If they're so successful, why can't they find my mom? Is it because she can't be found?

"But you won't be there?" I ask.

"Chin up. You don't need me, Ruby."

I can't help the way my eyes dart to the room across from mine. The one that went dark last night. Moving to another unit means it's not my turn to die. As much as that brings me peace, the thought of going somewhere else, with more people I don't know, makes my stomach hurt. But I can't give in to that. Because leaving here means I'm one step closer to getting out of the hospital. I didn't come here to die.

"When am I going?"

"After breakfast."

I set my spoon to the side of the bowl. Push it across the tray. "I'm ready."

Nurse Cathy comes to my side. "You're a fighter, Ruby Babcock." She unwraps my arm bandage and dabs on a fresh coat of ointment. I dare a glance at the rack of stitches. My cut is red and angry. A reminder of the rubble. "You'll have a scar." She fastens the self-stick tape at the end of the bandage, rests her hand above my elbow. "Let yours remind you of how brave you've been. How brave you are."

"I'll try."

She takes off her gloves. Drops them into the red hazardous-waste bin. Heads back to the workstation and into my room again with clothes in her hands.

"I found a clean sweatshirt and sweatpants and some sneakers in the donation box. You can change before you go." She sets them down on my bed along with a T-shirt for a 5K marathon I'll never run and a big pair of clean white underwear like my grandma might wear.

"Like the first day of school," I say. She laughs.

She gives me privacy to change, then helps me into a wheelchair. She puts my dirty team sweatshirt and Charlie's journal into a plastic bag and sets it on my lap. I look down at myself and instantly remember a photo of my mom and dad leaving the hospital with me after I was born. She's sitting in a wheelchair like this one, but instead of holding a plastic bag with a dirty sweatshirt, she's holding me. I am pink and tiny and wrapped in a blanket. My mom looks unsure. My dad looks proud.

"Ready?"

I nod.

The pod people stand and wave farewell as we go by. Even though they're strangers, they're happy for my recovery. The Big One has connected all of us.

Nurse Cathy pushes me toward the elevator. Punches the button with her knuckle. "Good news: the elevators are running again. Progress."

I remember the way the men from the ambulance brought me through the stairwell, passing the bodies piled up. I remember the stench and my being afraid I'd be one of them. Because of Nurse Cathy and Doctor Patel and the man with the big hands and the calm voice, I'm not.

The bright lights inside the elevator make Nurse Cathy look extra tired.

"Do you get to go home after this?"

She shrugs. "Unlikely. The work is endless. I've been catching a couple of hours of sleep at the hospital when I can."

"I'm glad you took care of me." I need to say the words because I want her to know them. I want her to know I'm thankful for her.

She smiles. "I am too."

The elevator dings, the doors slide open, and Nurse Cathy wheels me through some big doors on another floor. It doesn't even look like a regular hospital corridor. It's just a big room, like an auditorium, full of cots and people. Young people. Little kids. Kids who are whimpering. Some curled into their own bodies, sucking their thumbs. Others my age, sitting in corners or gathered around the big window in the back. There's a crack through the middle of the window. A jagged and uneven scar like the one on my arm. A reminder that this building shook but didn't break.

"I have Ruby Babcock for you," Nurse Cathy says to another nurse who wears white scrubs with teddy bears on them.

"Nice to meet you, Ruby. I'm Nurse Yvette."

I'm holding Nurse Cathy's hand even though I don't remember reaching for it. "It's hard to say goodbye to you."

She crouches next to me. Meets me eye-to-eye. "This is a happy goodbye, Ruby. You'll be out of here in no time."

I hope she's right.

CHAPTER THIRTY-FIVE

9:45 A.M.

I SET MY SWEATSHIRT ONTO A COT TO CLAIM it. It's sandwiched between two other cots, one with a little boy, his arm in a sling, the other with a little girl. They can't be more than five years old. Kindergartners. Like Cathy's twins.

"Hi," I say.

They look at me with big eyes. Do they even know what's going on? Why isn't someone sitting with them? Holding their hands. Hushing their fears. I want to know how long they've been here but I don't want to ask questions that could scare them. Make them miss their moms in the same way I miss mine.

"What's your name?" the little girl asks. "I'm Valentina. That's Gregory."

"I'm Ruby."

"Are you a grown-up?" Valentina says.

"Not quite."

"Oh. I hoped you were a grown-up."

"You're tall," Gregory says. "I'm tall too. For my age." He stands up straight. Puffs his chest. "See?"

"Yep. Super tall."

I smile. Valentina smiles back at me. Her mouth is like a little heart. She has the perfect name.

I should stay with them. Comfort them. Be like Nurse Cathy. But I want to look out the window. I want to run to it. See outside. Know what's there.

"I'm going to go peek out the window."

"Can we come?" Gregory asks.

"Please?" Valentina begs.

I wonder how long they've been here. Is this room the only thing they've seen?

"Okay," I say.

I walk to the window, wringing my hands, nervous to get closer to the glass. Afraid to see. It hits me too late that I probably shouldn't be taking two little kids anywhere near it. As I get closer, I'm offered a view of the building next door. Another hospital tower with mirrored windows and people inside. Patients hooked up to machines. More doctors and nurses and static radios and blue-gray lights. More stairwells. More hallways.

I finally get close enough to see the ground below. I expect chaos. I expect everything to look like the laundromat. But from up here, the white tops of triage tents in the parking lot almost look peaceful, like beach towels spread out on the sand. The edges of them flap in the wind like kites. I remember Nurse Cathy saying this hospital is far from the epicenter. That it didn't sustain as much damage. Maybe the crack in the window in front of me is the worst of it. Because I don't see broken buildings and piles of cement on the ground. Here, there is only the horror of after. Empty triage tents. Rolled-over cots. Piles of trash. Hundreds of scattered folding chairs. Cars parked askew, like they'd arrived in a panic.

And then.

In the distance.

Tucked along the edge of the building and away from the front door, like they hoped nobody would notice, are rows and rows of bodies covered in sheets. I'm sick. Frozen.

Valentina pulls on my hand. I'm glad she's not tall enough to see. I hope she doesn't ask me to lift her up.

Instead she says, "Look at that bird over there." My gaze follows to where she's pointing at the window ledge on the building across the way. She never even thought to look anywhere else. "Is it a toucan?"

Gregory jumps up and down. "I wanna see!"

Valentina shows him where to look.

"Is it a toucan?" he asks me.

I want more than anything for it to be a toucan. I want Valentina and Gregory to witness something extraordinary today. But I also can't lie about reality.

"It's a pigeon," I say. An everyday bird doing an everyday thing.

I brace myself for their disappointment.

"Oooh! I love those!" Valentina coos.

"Me too!" Gregory pretends to take a photo using his hands as a camera.

I smile to myself. Because in that moment, I wish I could be five years old.

"Who wants to play Go Fish?" Gregory points at a nearby table and its collection of cards and board games.

Valentina flutters her fingers under her chin in excitement. "Will you play with us, Ruby?"

"Sure."

She drags me by my hand to the table.

As Gregory sorts the cards, I glimpse the cover of a worn-out *LA Times* newspaper sticking out from underneath a Monopoly box. It's dated from two days ago, and a wave of nausea washes over me as I read the headline: *Southern California Rocked by Catastrophic 7.8-Mag Quake.* And then the photos. Gutted buildings. Fires. Collapsed freeway overpasses. Firefighters running through the streets with the broken bodies of children cradled in their arms.

I grab the paper. Read the details.

The quake started near the US–Mexico border and threaded its way along hundreds of miles of the southern San Andreas Fault, leaving damage from San Diego County to the Salton Sea and Los Angeles County in its wake. The death toll is currently at eleven hundred but is anticipated to double. An estimated eighteen thousand have been injured, with new victims flooding hospitals by the hour. The water supply is limited due to damage to a main aqueduct. Multiple wildfires and structure fires have burned throughout the southern portion of the state, and many are still burning. Property damage is in the hundred billions. Southern California's infrastructure has basically collapsed as aftershocks continue to rock an already-fragile situation.

There isn't a safe space anywhere. Not on a freeway or a bridge or in a house or an office building or at the beach.

I'm instantly there. In that cold, dark space. With Charlie barely breathing. And the tiny sliver of light that came and went.

I can't look anymore. I shut the paper, toss it on the floor next to my feet, and focus on the cards Gregory hands me.

CHAPTER THIRTY-SIX

2:10 P.M.

AFTER LUNCH, I HAVE A VISITOR. SHE'S A CASE-worker from the hospital and she's here to help. That's her greeting: *I'm Miriam and I'm here to help.*

Her words are a relief. My shoulders decompress. I'm at a hospital far from home. A whole hour away. Far from the laundromat. Far from school. Far from my mom's office. But Miriam is here to help.

She pulls out a clipboard. "What's your full name?"

"Ruby Elizabeth Babcock."

She asks for my address and date of birth. And a whole bunch of other basic stuff. But I only want to know one thing.

"How will you find my mom?"

She asks me where my mom works and if we have the same last name. "When did you last speak to her?" Miriam asks.

"At dinner. The night before the earthquake." I don't tell her the details. I don't want Miriam to know one of the last things I said to my mom was that she'd ruined my life.

My eyes fill with tears. What if I never get to take it back?

Valentina sits down next to me. Pats my knuckles. "It's okay." I squeeze her hand. She shouldn't have to comfort me. She's just a little kid. "Can you give her one of your candies?" she asks Miriam. "It'll make her feel better."

Valentina already knows the drill. How long ago did she talk to Miriam? How many days have they been looking for her mom?

Miriam reaches into her pocket. Pulls out two Tootsie Pops. One grape. One orange. I'm suddenly on the bleachers at the football field with Leo, looking out at the earthquake drill we did on campus. I choke on a sob because I want to be there now. Where things were simpler. When I knew where my mom was.

Miriam hands me a tissue. Smiles sympathetically. "I know it feels like a lot. I'm asking you to please be patient. Things are taking a long time because everything is haywire right now."

Haywire is an odd word. Something you say when you're frazzled. Like when your backpack rips and your internet goes down so you can't send your AP English paper through Google Docs and you can't find your phone all at the same time.

Haywire is a simple problem. *Haywire* isn't what you call *this*.

But Miriam is here to help me, so I say, "Okay. I understand." Because at least it's something. At least it's hope.

"Trust me, I want you to find your mom as much as you do, Ruby. We just have to take it one step at a time."

ONE STEP AT A TIME

About six weeks ago, on the first morning back at practice after New Year's Eve, we were stretching on the pool deck before getting in the water. Mila groaned in protest every time she had to move her body, and the team laughed it off like she was merely doing it to entertain us.

I knew better.

I recognized a Mila hangover when I saw it.

But we'd had a best-friend breakup a few days before, right? And she hadn't made any contact with me since then. Not a single text, or Snap, or heart on Instagram. Still, I was worried she could get in trouble showing up to practice the way she was. On top of everything, she was our star goalie with an all-league status and we needed her. We didn't have a shot at the championship without her.

I tried angling my body in front of Mila when Coach walked over to give us our usual two-minute warning that it was time to get in the water.

My position was awkward. Uncomfortable. Too obvious.

Coach looked at me funny, tilting his head to the side and squinting his eyes. "You okay there, Babcock?"

"Yep." I stretched my arms behind my back and looked the other way.

Just then, Mila lost her balance, stumbled into me, and

took us both down to the ground. It was New Year's Eve on the beach all over again. I pictured Robert hovering above us. Leering. Creepy. I scrambled to untangle myself from Mila and she kicked me in the stomach. Hard.

"Oh my god!" I shouted. "Stop!"

"Get off me," she said, flailing her arms. "I'm gonna barf."

How many times in my life had I watched Mila get sick from drinking? Too many to count.

She jumped to her feet and ran to the nearest trash can in time to hurl up her breakfast. Her liquid breakfast. I could smell the alcohol from ten feet away. Coach must've smelled it, too.

"What the . . . Have you been drinking?!" he yelled.

Mila shook her head, but the effort of it must've hurt because she pressed her thumbs to her temples.

Juliette piped in. "She's sick, Coach. It's going around. My mom had it over break."

Lie. Not true. But I wasn't the only one on the team who'd spent the last year covering for Mila. It was in our blood. Teamwork.

Coach turned to Juliette. "Nice try, but I wasn't born yesterday."

Mila leaned over the trash can and threw up again. We all turned our backs, trying to tame our gag reflexes.

"Mila," Coach said, "go sleep it off. I don't want to see you on my pool deck like this again." He grabbed her duffel bag to hand it to her, but one of the handles slipped from his grip. The unzipped mouth of the bag opened wide and out rolled a half-empty glass bottle of tequila. We all froze as it tumbled across the concrete, coming to a stop against the bleachers.

Coach bent down. Picked it up. Spun it in his hand.

"It's not mine," Mila whimpered, still clutching the edges of the trash can to steady herself.

Coach didn't tear his eyes away from Mila. "You. Come with me." And then, "The rest of you. Get in the water."

"Oh, god," Mila mumbled. "It's not mine."

We all stood there, mouths agape, watching Coach Sanchez march Mila off the pool deck and to the principal's office.

Before they passed through the gate, Coach turned to us again. "I said get in the water!"

We scrambled, tucking our hair into swim caps and securing our goggles across our faces. I was the first one in, moving up and down the lane for warm-up laps, staring at that black line along the bottom of the pool as a million thoughts ran through my head.

She'd said the bottle wasn't hers.

But it was in her duffel bag with her name embroidered on it.

She could be in a lot of trouble.

But it's her first offense.

She'll likely only be suspended.

Coach returned alone about halfway through practice and didn't say a word. Didn't give us any hint of what had happened in the principal's office. We finished our workout, showered, and headed to class. I lingered at my locker, waiting to see if Mila would show up in the hallway.

She didn't.

By lunchtime, it was clear she was gone.

And by the end of the school day, right before afternoon practice, her one-word text came through to Iris:

Expelled.

DAY EIGHT

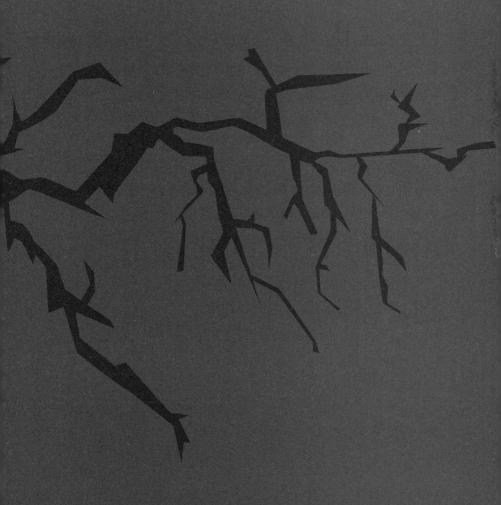

FRIDAY

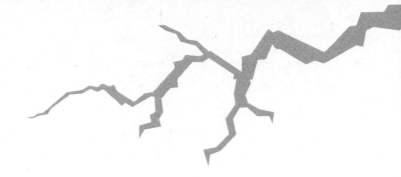

CHAPTER THIRTY-SEVEN

8:30 A.M.

THERE'S A CRASH. AND A BANG LOUD ENOUGH to silence the murmurs that fill this space. A wail erupts from the hallway. I jump back when the heavy wood doors swing open and a woman about my mom's age shoves herself inside this auditorium that's been filled end-to-end, cot-to-cot. She has haggard hair. She is frantic and frazzled in mismatched clothes. She looks like someone who has been walking and searching for days.

"Matthew! Are you here?"

Nurse Yvette shouts for help.

Valentina and Gregory whimper and pull the blankets up under their chins. I reach a hand out to each of them. Try to comfort.

A nurse attempts to calm the woman down with gentle hands and quiet shushes.

It doesn't stop her.

The woman pushes past the nurse, her eyes darting to empty corners and closed doors. Spinning around in desperation.

"I was told there are unclaimed minors here. Is Matthew here? Where's my son?" The woman fists her hands against her thighs, raises her face to the ceiling, and yells at the top of her lungs. "Matthew! Are you here? Matthew!"

An orderly moves in to try to calm the frantic woman. She shakes him with desperate strength.

"Stop it! I need to find my son!"

She is a mother who wants to tear down walls and scream in the middle of hospital corridors to find her kid. Even if it terrorizes every other kid who isn't hers.

The woman runs around the room, tearing blankets off the cots to see if Matthew is underneath them. So many kids are crying, and nurses rush around trying to console them. Shushing and telling them, "It's okay, it's okay," even though it's not.

Finally, a security guard wrestles Matthew's mom away, holding her tight with thick arms and a vice grip.

Someone else hurries to the woman. Raises her clipboard. "What's his name?" Another social worker like Miriam.

Matthew's mom's eyes are wild and unfocused. The woman says something closer to Matthew's mom's ear. It makes her stop fighting. The security guard loosens his grip. Matthew's mom puts her hands out to take the clipboard.

"What's his name?" the woman asks again, handing over the clipboard.

Matthew's mom hunches above it, blocking it with her whole body so nobody can take the clipboard from her. She pores over it methodically. Slow and deliberate until she gets to the end. And then she starts over again, ripping through the pages faster, running her fingertip back and forth.

Looking. Hoping. Wishing.

And when she's done, she tosses the clipboard. It lands with a clang against the floor of the room. The papers go flying.

"Where are you?!" she shouts, and falls to her knees. "My baby!" She rolls into herself like a ball. Clutches clumps of her hair and pulls. Her jacket bunches up around her feet like a petticoat. And then she lets out the most primal howl. It's a painful, wretched sound that I feel deep in my bones. It is the sound of a mother who has lost her child.

She rocks.

Back and forth she goes.

Pounding her hand against the floor. *Boom, boom* it echoes. A drumbeat. A plea. Repeating one word:

Matthew.

Matthew.

Matthew.

Her pain is too much to witness. It convinces me I have to go. I tuck Charlie's journal against my chest, pull my crusty sweatshirt over my head on top of the other sweatshirt I'm already wearing, and make for the door.

Another orderly turns toward me. Makes eye contact. Scrunches his brow. "Where are you going?" he says.

Matthew's mom howls again while kids stand frozen with fear.

There is only one thing I can do.

Run.

CHAPTER THIRTY-EIGHT

8:40 A.M.

I WILL NOT TAKE NO FOR AN ANSWER TODAY.

I can't stay here and do nothing anymore.

I won't.

If Matthew's mom can find her way across the city to look for her son, I can do the same to find my mom. Nurse Cathy and Miriam and the newspapers made it seem impossible to find people, but there has to be a way. First I have to get out of here. So my mom doesn't get lost like Matthew.

I round several corners and end up in a hallway like the one I waited in when I got here. My skin pulsing with heat and fever and fear. It seems like years ago. I wade through the muddled masses of cots and people. I can't help but see their burnt, dirty faces. Their arms and legs scratched and torn. They are bruised and broken. They cry. Bleed. Groan.

I was here. I was this.

I study every person I pass. Because what if my mom is here? What if Leo is here? Or my friends? Is this where I should start my search?

A doctor bumps my shoulder as he navigates a teen girl on a stretcher through the crowd. She grits her teeth in pain. Her eyes dart. I sense her fear. I remember my own when I waited here, not knowing anyone. Not knowing if I was okay. Convinced hospitals are where people go to die so it must be my turn. But I made it because of Nurse Cathy and the man with the big hands and the calm voice and Doctor Patel. And me. Because of that, I'm okay and my room belongs to someone else now. Maybe this girl will go to a room like the one I had and be Doctor Patel's next patient.

She needs to know this is a good thing.

"It's okay," I say to her. She looks for my voice. I'm sure she wishes it were coming from someone she knows. I can't give her that. But I can try to give her peace. Hope. "Everyone is here to help. Let them help."

And then she is around the corner. Gone. So I push forward.

Still checking every stretcher and doorway for someone I know. Someone I love.

An old man reaches for me. Wants to knot my fingers with his the same way I wanted to knot mine with Charlie's. I fold his hand into mine as I pass, thinking I'll give him a brief moment of comfort, then move on. But when I look at his face, he looks back at me with watery eyes. His skin hangs ashen and dull.

He's almost gone.

"Nurse!" I yell, waving my free hand. "Over here! Hurry!"

The nurse rushes over. Puts her fingertips to his wrist. Checks his pulse. I hold his other hand, waiting. Hoping. The nurse shakes her head. Mouths, "I'm sorry."

What? "No." My eyes tear. They can't just pick and choose. "Do something!"

But she moves on. Eager to help someone who still has a chance.

This man doesn't.

The old man's fingers loosen their grip on mine. He gasps for breath. I hang on tighter. He's slipping but I can't let go. Nobody deserves to die all alone in a hallway. I remember Charlie. The way he stayed with Jason at the fraternity party, waiting for the ambulance, holding on to hope. I told him it mattered that he'd stayed with him until the end. It mattered that Charlie didn't let his friend die alone.

"I'm here," I say. I want to give this man something. Access to a memory. A vision better than here. But I don't know him. I don't know his life.

So I tell him about the things I love. That most people love. Like sunshine and ocean water and salty air and sandy feet. His breathing strains. It's the sound of Charlie all over again. I close my eyes. Try to give him what I couldn't give Charlie. I tighten my grip on his hand. Let him know the feel of skin on skin from another human in his final moments. I keep talking.

Of blue skies and tall mountains. Of love and laughter. Of the first day of summer. And the last day of winter. Of clouds and air. Of trees and flowers.

"Margaret . . ." The word is a whisper. "Loves flowers."

"Yes, Margaret does love flowers. She's picking flowers now. She's in a great big field of them. There are so many colors. It's so beautiful. She's happy. She loves you. So much."

The tiniest flicker of a smile edges the corner of his mouth as his watery eyes focus then fade.

One last breath.

His hand goes still in mine.

And he's gone.

I want to fall to the floor like the woman in the yellow shirt. Not just for this man but for Charlie, too. And his friend at the fraternity party. And the person in the bed in the room across from mine in the ICU. For the rows of people lined up along the outside of the hospital and inside the stairwells. For the ones covered up in the triage tents and the ones who won't be found.

But I have to keep moving. I have to keep pushing myself forward, one foot in front of the other. So I rest this man's hand over the still space of his heart and let go.

I don't want to risk waiting for an elevator and being greeted by security guards when I make it to the first floor, so I take a breath, pull Charlie's journal against my chest, adjust my sweatshirt collar over my mouth and nose, and push the heavy door open into the stairwell.

Don't look, I tell myself. *Don't breathe.*

The bodies are still piled there. More now than before. The rotting smell even worse. My eyes sting and my lungs scream as I run downstairs, passing all of them as I round each flight.

It seems to go on forever.

Until. Finally. An exit door.

I push it open and stumble into the cold morning air, gasping for breath. My head spins, dizzy, from running down multiple flights of stairs without breathing. I steady myself against the side of the building. Inhale fresh air. Try to focus. What if I'm not healed enough to do this? My knees wobble and my vision blurs. I squint my eyes against the daylight. It's overcast but still so bright compared to the rubble and the blue-gray dim of hospital rooms. But I'm out here in it. I made it. I raise my face to the sky. Let the wind take hold of my hair. To remind me I'm alive. That I survived. And when I finally feel the fizz in my fingertips fade, I push off the wall and move on.

Tents clutter the parking lot. So many people still need help. Then I see a table stacked with granola bars and bottled waters. I edge closer. Not granola bars. Protein bars. Like the ones packed in my emergency earthquake kit in elementary school. I take exactly five. I can make them last for two to three days. Taking more would feel like stealing from the volunteers. Or the ones still hurting. The ones still healing. I stuff the bars and four water bottles into the pockets of my sweatshirt. Then go.

CHAPTER THIRTY-NINE

9:20 A.M.

I RIP OPEN A PROTEIN BAR AND TAKE A BITE.
It's chewy like caramel, but not nearly as delicious. Chocolate,
I think. Chocolate mixed with cardboard. It sticks to my teeth.
Feels filmy on my tongue. But I keep eating because I know it will
give me the strength I need.

I walk through the gray morning mist of the marine layer and
anxiously await the bright streaks of sunshine to burn through.
They're arriving slowly but surely, sputtering to a start. The sky
goes orange with beginning.

I look up at the dangling sign of a freeway overpass. Take note
of the next exit written on the sign. It's one I know from traveling
on school buses to water polo games. I'm inland. I'm closer to the
foothills than I am to my mom's office. I need to head west.

I change course. Walk on.

By the time I come upon a makeshift shelter in the middle of the grass field of a park a few blocks later, my stomach is begging for another protein bar. I sip water instead. Watch the people. They're living in tents or out of their cars, their belongings stuffed into laundry baskets and trash bags. The energy is restless. Furtive. Most people gather in circles of trust around their stuff. I stick to the fringe to let them know I'm a stranger. A few feet from me, a disheveled woman hunches over a hibachi grill. No food. Just heat. Three small kids huddle behind her. One of them is an infant, not even walking yet. He isn't wearing pants or a diaper, only a dirty T-shirt. Another is a little girl, probably five years old, with uneven ponytails and stained pants. Her brother, next to her, is younger and wearing stripes. The kids look hungry. Cold. I wish I'd looked for more things around that table in the hospital parking lot. Maybe there were diapers. Blankets. Toothbrushes. Food. Soap. Things I could give to people who need them.

"Hello," I say to the woman. Testing the waters. The fact that she's a mom makes her seem safer to approach than the other strangers. But then she looks at me. Narrows her eyes. Gathers her children behind the protective fold of her back.

"What?" she says, firm with warning.

I hesitate. "I wanted to tell you, there's a table back at the hospital. There's food. Water. There's help."

I take a step toward her and she angles her body closer to the grill. Too close. I'm afraid her hair will catch fire. She grits her teeth. Looks at me hard.

"I have a gun," she says, but doesn't make a move for it.

I falter. Put my hands up. "I don't want anything."

"Everyone wants something."

"I don't. Really. I just want to help." But that's not entirely true. Because I do want something. I want information. I want to know what she knows about getting to the parts of town beyond here. Back to Pacific Shore. Back to home. "I'm trying to find my mom."

Her face softens. I think it again. *She's a mom. She knows.* But in an instant she stiffens her shoulders again. Precisely because she is a mom. Her own kids come first.

I get it. I do.

My mom would do the same for me.

The baby peeks out from behind her back. Shivers. She pulls him in front of her. Gathers him in her lap. Tries to warm him by rubbing her hands up and down his bare legs. I remember the cold of the rubble. The way my teeth chattered and my fingertips froze. Her baby is cold like I was. And right now I'm almost too warm in all these layers.

"Do you want my sweatshirt?" I ask.

She studies my filthy team sweatshirt, crusty with dried blood. "You keep it."

I shake my head. "No, no. Not this one." When I walked into the laundromat, I was thinking about quitting water polo. I gave my championship ring to Charlie, but I hung on to my sweatshirt. It stopped the bleeding in my arm and told Nurse Cathy where I'm from. I wouldn't give up this sweatshirt. I empty the pockets and line the protein bars and bottled waters at my feet, along with

Charlie's journal. I unzip my dirty team sweatshirt and point to the soft gray sweatshirt from the hospital underneath. "But you can have this one."

Her baby shivers in her lap. The little girl behind her sneezes. I pull the clean sweatshirt off, still warm from my body heat, and hold it out to this mom while I stand in the 5K T-shirt. She hesitates. Until her baby whimpers. And then she quickly grabs the sweatshirt from me and wraps him in it.

She nods. "Thank you. That's . . . incredibly generous."

I zip up my dirty sweatshirt. Tuck Charlie's journal underneath. Bend to collect my food.

"Mommy, I'm thirsty," the older boy says, eyeing my water.

His words send me straight to the rubble. When I got water and Charlie didn't. I tried to direct it his way, knowing he was as thirsty as I was, but it never got to him. I hold tight to one of my water bottles. I couldn't help Charlie. But I can help this little boy now. I hold the bottle out to him. He looks at his mom, asking permission to take it. She looks at me.

"Are you sure? Don't you need it?"

"You need it more. I just need to find my mom."

"Go ahead," she says to her son. Then to me, as her eyes glisten, "Thank you. Again. Thank you." She untwists the cap. Rations their gulps so there's something for everyone.

"I need to go. I need to figure out how to get back home."

She points right. "If you walk about five blocks that way, you'll be on the main drag. You'll have better luck finding help to get you where you're going."

"Five blocks?"

She nods.

"Thanks."

I turn to go.

"Hey," she calls out to me after I've taken a few steps. I stop. Turn back around to face her. "There's been looting over there. Arrests. If you were my daughter, I'd want someone to tell you to be careful. So for your mom, I'm saying it. Be careful."

"I will."

I walk five blocks. Round the corner. See the police cars. Hear a police officer shouting from a megaphone.

"This street is closed," he says. "Use alternate routes or risk arrest."

It doesn't feel safe here. There's almost a palpable crackle to the air, telling me to turn around. I know there's been looting because entire televisions are in the middle of the sidewalk. Dropped. Broken. And then the more necessary things like boxes of diapers, baby formula, and empty jugs of water. On top of that is the trash and discarded remnants of the things that became too much to carry. Chairs. Laptops. Plastic crates full of treasured belongings. Things from home.

Where was everyone going? Where are they now?

I recognize the hollowed-out storefronts of this main street. My mom and I have taken weekend day trips here to shop and have lunch and see a movie. The places I know are hard to recognize now among the broken windows and debris.

A siren sounds, and about ten people come running toward

me. My heartbeat amps up as I get caught in the tangle of them. I turn and run with them to avoid whatever they're fleeing. Tear gas? Guns? I run three blocks, trying to escape the chaos, then stop at the corner, bent over and dragging in air. Like Charlie in the rubble. Like the old man in the hallway. I should sit down and rest. Figure out a plan.

My mom's office is at least a thirty-minute car ride from here. There's no way I'll have the strength to make it on foot. What parts of me will I have to abandon along the way?

I duck into a doorway when I see a police officer with her back to me on the sidewalk ahead. I hold my breath. Wait until she goes away.

It feels good to stop moving, so I sink to the dirty ground. I unscrew the top off a bottled water and down it in one take. I tell myself five minutes. A little time to rest and regain my strength.

STRONG

I drove beach roads in California. Bumper-to-bumper on hot summer days or in the evening rush. Past bright orange sunsets, surfers, and sandy-footed tourists eating ice-cream cones.

But the beach in winter was different.

In the winter, the fog rolled in and the pale blue lifeguard towers were shuttered, standing still like tiny houses on the sand. Bracing for the cold. Looking lonely. Looking sad. There weren't any tourists in their wrinkled-from-the-suitcase clothes with their sunburns and their floppy hats.

On the Fourth of July, when I first talked to Leo and got jittery at the feel of his shoulder touching mine, the beach was warm and crowded and full of life. Buzzing with energy and promise.

But a couple weekends ago, when we walked down the pier and stared out at the big waves, it was empty. Cloudy and dull. We passed only one person—a woman pushing a dog wearing sunglasses in a stroller.

"Sometimes I can't believe we live in this town," I said, watching her pass.

"We'll miss it when we're gone."

"Do you think so?"

"I know so."

"I think I'll miss this. Us. The fact that you can be right here whenever."

He laughed.

"What? It's true," I said. "Like when you're somewhere and I'm somewhere else, we won't be able to just walk down to the beach and laugh at dogs in sunglasses."

"I think we'll live."

I chuckled. "You know what I mean."

"We'll be good. We'll be better than good."

"You think?"

"I know."

"Okay."

We walked down the stairs of the pier. Sat side by side in the cold sand. The waves roared in, pummeling the shore in their wintry, angry strength.

Leo reached for me. Grazed my fingers with his. I gave his hand a squeeze then stood up and walked to the water. I dipped my naked toes in the wetness. Felt the cold foam fizzle until Leo came up behind me, laughing.

"You have a day off from practice, but you can't stay out of the water," he said.

He leaned in to nuzzle my neck. Turned me around. Kissed me sweetly. Even though my feet were numb from the ocean, I felt that kiss all the way to my toes.

I dug my feet in deeper. Let them sink into the heavy wet sand. I wanted the waves to cover all of me. To keep us forever.

I looked at the water in front of me. Thought of all the

faraway places it could take us. All the places my mom and dad had seen.

I remembered her telling me how she'd sat on the same beach before I was born. She stepped into the same ocean with me in her stomach and my dad at her side. The first time she ever felt me kick was when the cold water hit her bare belly. Like I knew we were beach people and I was aware I was home.

It's where she took me on the day my dad was buried when I was four months old. A few hours before, she'd stood by his grave, listened to the hollow thump of dirt shoveled over his coffin, feeling helpless. And scared. And so suddenly alone. All she wanted to do was feel the ocean. So she left a full house of the people who loved her most. Her friends and coworkers. Roommates from college. The neighbors from two doors down. My mom's mom and my dad's sister and brother. His parents, aunts, and uncles. All those people who knew my dad best. They had spent the afternoon making pity faces at my mom while putting their hands on her wet cheeks and promising they'd be there if she needed them. If she needed anything, they would be her people. No matter what or when or where.

She said thank you because that's what you say when people make promises like that. But after she'd said thank you one time too many, she darted past a table full of casserole dishes and untouched desserts.

She went to her room, put on her bikini, and snuck out the back door with me.

She walked us to the beach.

Ran barefoot through the hot sand.

Dropped her towel down.

Made her way into the water with me in her arms.

The water licked at her toes. Rolled over her feet. Crept up her ankles. Pushing. Pulling. She kept moving forward because moving forward was what she had to do.

A million thoughts swirling. A million *what if*s and *how*s and *why*s running through her head.

I've heard that story so many times. I know it like my own because it's the moment that made us.

It's the story about how she wasn't sure she could raise me all by herself.

But then she dipped my toes into the water and I squealed. I kicked my feet, splashing her with the salty ocean water as I laughed. And then she said she understood.

I was meant to be.

I was a piece of my dad left behind.

We would be a team.

She would do everything she could to protect me.

She would be strong.

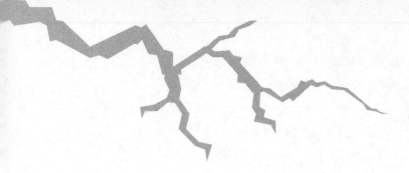

CHAPTER FORTY

10:48 A.M.

WHEN I OPEN MY EYES, A GIRL WATCHES me, blocking my exit to the doorway to the street. She looks my age, swimming in a pair of overalls, her long hair hanging in a sloppy braid behind her back. Her gaze drifts to the pile of protein bars and my last water bottle that fell free from my pockets while I rested. I lunge forward on my knees. Scoop them up and shove them back into my sweatshirt. I'm that mom at the park. Protecting her kids and her hibachi grill.

"Chill," the girl says, putting her hands up and taking a step away. "I'm not going after your food."

I scramble back, the concrete wall scraping my shoulder so much like the rubble.

"I'm Ava," she says. "Just wanted to check on you. You okay?"

I lift my head. Check in with myself. My arm doesn't hurt. I'm tired but my head is clear. I sit up straight. Square my shoulders. "I'm fine."

"So what's your deal? Are you lost?"

"A little," I say.

"What's that mean?"

"I know where I am but I don't know how to get to where I need to go."

"Which is where?"

"Pacific Shore. My mom's there." I hope.

She tightens a loose strap on her overalls. "Look, I can help you if you want." She nods over her shoulder. "We have a van. It's not the greatest—you'd have to sit on the floor in the back—but it's running and my brother and I can take you somewhere if you're up for it."

"Would you get in some random van with you and your brother if you were me?"

She laughs. "I know it sounds totally sketch, but I swear we're legit. We just dropped off waters at a shelter and took home some dude who got stuck across town."

"What shelter?"

"Red Cross shelter. At the gym at Francis Middle School."

That does sound legit, but getting in a van with people I don't know isn't the same as getting in an ambulance or going to a hospital ward for kids who can't find their parents. The people helping in those places were the people you'd expect to be helping. Two teenagers in the middle of a street full of police cars and looters doesn't seem like the same thing. But this might be my only chance to get to my mom.

"Your parents are cool with that? I'm pretty sure my mom wouldn't be," I say.

She shrugs. "Our parents taught us everything we know."

"Are they with you?"

"Nope. They're disaster volunteers for the Red Cross, so they're helping out at the shelter by our house."

"So it's just you and your brother?"

"Yep. Just me and Luke."

She waves to him. He's standing next to a white van that doesn't have any back windows and is raised up on monster-truck tires that would crush my mom's Prius in five seconds. It's basically the poster child for the kind of van you should never get into.

I watch as Luke lifts a gallon jug of water to his mouth and gulps, his long, shaggy beach hair hanging over his shoulders. The side door of the van is open, and I twist my body to peek inside. I see cases of water and big boxes of snacks like the ones you'd get at Costco. It seems like Ava's telling the truth. Like they're driving around, helping people and distributing food.

I give in. "Okay." Accepting help is my choice this time. "Thanks."

CHAPTER FORTY-ONE

10:55 A.M.

"NEXT STOP, PACIFIC SHORE," AVA TELLS HER
brother. "Ruby needs to find her mom."

He grins at me. "I take it you're Ruby?"

I nod. "I am. Thanks for helping."

"No worries. I'm Luke, by the way."

"I know. Ava told me what the two of you have been doing. I'm impressed."

He shrugs the same way Ava did. The same way Nurse Cathy did about working all week. Like they wouldn't have it any other way. And like it's nothing that deserves special attention, even though I think it does.

"Ready?" Ava asks me.

I nod and climb into the back of the van. It's not a cushy minivan with DVD players and automatic sliding doors like my friends' parents drove us around in when we were kids. It's more like a delivery van. There aren't even seats in the back. So I settle onto the hard metal floor as Ava buckles herself into the driver's seat and Luke settles into the passenger seat with a pile of road maps in his lap.

"Old-school navigation," he tells me.

The back of the van smells faintly of surf wax, a reminder of Luke and Ava's life before The Big One, but right now it's stuffed with tarps and blankets instead of surfboards. Also food and water. Canned goods. Baby formula. Unopened packages of socks and underwear. Plus the empty wrappers of what they've already eaten themselves. My mouth waters at a box of snack-bag chips.

"Stop it," I say.

Ava turns around, alarmed. Like I'm hurt. "What?"

"Sorry. I'm fine. But . . . would it be obnoxious if I asked for Cheetos?"

Luke laughs. "Go for it."

I rip into a bag like I've never had junk food in my life. When the first taste of orange cheese powder hits my tongue, I literally moan with relief. It's so simple. Normal. I should savor them, but I don't. I down the whole bag in seconds, then lick the remnant cheese dust from my fingertips. Part of me wants to turn the bag inside out and lick that, too.

The van bounces hard over a big bump, and I almost bite my own finger. I grab tight on to the back of Luke's seat to steady myself.

"Sorry," Ava says. "Lotsa road damage."

"I can handle it," I say. "It's better than being in the back of an ambulance, thinking I'm going to die."

"Ambulance? What the hell? Are you okay?" Ava asks.

I make a fist, and no pain shoots to my wound. "I think so."

The van's wheels seem rugged and made for rough terrain. Like they can drive through places other cars wouldn't be able to go. I keep a hold on Luke's seat as I'm jostled, my whole body protesting the quick movements. My feet bounce against the floor and I sway. I hope I don't get carsick.

"Try to make the next left," Luke says, looking at his map. "And a right after that."

I suck in a breath when we pass two dead bodies in the gutter, like someone just needed to move them out of the way and keep going.

Luke twists to look at me. "Is this the first time you're seeing stuff like that?"

"Yeah. I mean, I was in the hospital. I saw things there." Bodies in stairwells. And lined up along the side of the building. "But I didn't think I'd see . . . in the middle of the street."

"Better get used to it," Luke says.

Ava slams on the brakes.

I lose my grip on Luke's seat and bang into the box of canned goods. It pummels my shoulders but keeps me from sliding all the way to the back of the van.

"Shit. Sorry," Ava says.

I scramble up, regain my grip on Luke's seat, and look out the front window to see what stopped Ava. The street has split, leaving a cavernous hole in its wake.

"Whoa."

"What do I do?" Ava asks Luke.

He looks at his map, holding his fingertip in place to mark where we are. "Back up. Turn left."

We reverse to the first corner behind us and turn. It looks like we're clear for a while. But then the van climbs a hill and the dilapidated sprawl is everywhere.

My town. My home. My life. My rubble.

Roads are split in two, and tar buckles like a wavy ribbon where the neat, yellow-painted line should be. Stop signs bend into the street. Traffic lights don't flash. I pull my hand to my mouth, stunned into silence as we get closer and closer to the places I recognize. Where buildings I know are burned-out and blackened. Some slanted. Others are hollowed-out shells. More of them are pieces toppled over on top of one another. The Pacific Shore Movie Theater, where Leo and I saw a midnight screening of *The Rocky Horror Picture Show*. The DMV, where I took my driving test.

Are people still trapped inside? Crushed? Dead? Dying?

We drive toward an overpass scrunched up like an accordion. The prongs of the wire fence that would normally run along its sides hang down like tendrils. Precarious. Ready to collapse. Cars have been abandoned in the middle of the road. Some of them are facing the wrong way. Blocking us. We can't go forward. We have to turn around and try yet another route.

"It's like a maze," Ava says, keeping her eyes on the road.

"Or a really screwed-up video game," Luke says, eyes on the map. "But we're getting better at figuring it out."

And then we're driving past my school. It's Friday. Classes should be in session. I should be in third period analyzing Mary Shelley's *Frankenstein*. My hair in a bun, still damp and smelling like chlorine from morning practice.

"This is my school," I say, gripping one side each of Ava's and Luke's seats.

Luke rolls down his window. The air smells like chemicals, dust, and blackened smoke. The marquee that's usually lit up with the constant scroll of good news and important dates is blown out and bent over like the stop signs. The sidewalks are empty of gardeners with leaf blowers or classmates with backpacks and skateboards and Starbucks cups. Entire buildings are no more. Their guts crumbled to the ground. Their skeleton bones scattered.

"Ours looks about the same," Ava says.

"Which school?"

"Ocean View."

"I know your school. We've played you in water polo." I can see their campus and their pool and their hallways. The blue-and-white school-record banners.

"We haven't seen a high school that doesn't look like ours," Luke says. "But Harbor's the worst of all of them. They had a fire. Burned everything to the ground."

Harbor. Charlie's high school. *Charlie.* I press his journal to my chest.

"I had a friend who went to Harbor." I knot my hands in my lap. "He was with me before I got rescued. He didn't make it, but I don't know if anyone knows he's there. I want his family to know. I'm sure they're looking, and I can only imagine how worried they must be."

"Maybe we can do something." Ava looks to Luke. "Can we?"

Luke shrugs. "We can ask Mom."

"I can tell you his name," I say, my voice ticking up with relief. "The laundromat where we were. He went to Harbor and then Stanford." My words are tumbling out in a hurry to tell Charlie's story so it doesn't get lost to the rubble.

"If we have his name and know where he was, our mom will probably know what to do," Ava says. "Whether it's FEMA or the Red Cross, right, Luke?"

"I think so. We can definitely try."

"Done. It's our next assignment," Ava says.

"Really? Thank you."

We round the corner, and I see the makeshift emergency room on the football field. There are four tents set up same as they were for the earthquake drill I didn't take seriously enough. Where Mila fake-broke her leg and I ate a Tootsie Pop and Coach tagged the dead. I hope other people paid better attention than I did. And I hope it made all the difference and kept them safe.

Classes were done by the time The Big One hit, but there would've still been people on campus doing after-school activities. What happened to the soccer team on this very field? The ground looks fine, free of sinkholes, but there are downed wires and fallen debris from the cracked concrete bleachers. Was everybody okay, or were they the first ones dragged to these tents? Who went to the dead tent? Was Coach here? Did he come running from the pool deck to help? Or was he too hurt to go? Was he helping my teammates instead? I imagine everything broken and people underneath it all. Bloody. Barely breathing. Trapped. Like I was. And Charlie. I hear the screams of terror. I feel the fear.

It will always live here now.

I bend down to look through the windshield, eyes wide and unbelieving. Part of me wants to open the door and get out. To touch the devastation. To feel that it's real, because the sight of it is too hard to believe.

Ava slows the van to a crawl. Gives me time to look. How can everything we've ever known look like this?

It's a scene that erases hope.

"Go, please," I say, because I can't look anymore.

Ava pushes her foot to the gas pedal and the van lurches forward, inching up onto the sidewalk to drive around an orange plastic roadblock that takes up the whole crosswalk.

I grip the side of Luke's seat. "Are you allowed to go here?"

Ava shrugs. "There kind of aren't any rules anymore."

I direct them to my mom's office, but we can only get within a few blocks of it because the roads are too mangled. Ava kills the engine. Everything goes quiet, but my ears still buzz from the constant vibration of driving in the great big van.

"Can you get there from here?" Luke asks me.

I look out and around. The echo of chaos lives here just as

it has on every other street I've seen today, but I know where I am.

"I can get there," I say.

I open the heavy passenger-side door and jump out.

"Here," Luke says, handing me a pen and a pad of paper. I think of Charlie writing in his journal and feel the weight of it underneath my sweatshirt. I pull my hand to my stomach to remind me I'm still carrying his words. "Write down what you know about your friend."

I prop Luke's notebook on my knee and put down the things that matter. "His name was Charleston Smith," I tell him, "but he went by Charlie because he thought Charleston made him sound like an asshole."

Luke laughs. "I like him already."

"Right?" I try to keep from tearing up at the memory of my friend and hand the pad of paper back to Luke. "Please find him."

Ava nods her head at me. "We're on it, Ruby. Now *you* go find your mom."

"How do I even thank you for everything you did for me?"

"You don't," Luke says.

"One day you'll help someone else when they need it," Ava says.

CHAPTER FORTY-TWO

12:02 P.M.

WHEN I ROUND THE CORNER AND FIRST SEE the building that once housed my mom's office, it takes everything I have not to sink to the ground in despair. Ten stories have tumbled down. Bits and pieces sit crisscrossed on top of one another like pickup sticks.

There are rescue workers scattered and dogs poking around. There are trucks in the distance. There are tents. And people. But the insides of the tents are nearly empty. They aren't filled to capacity like the tents where the big hands and the calm voice brought me. I'm in the belly of downtown where there were so many people. It's day eight and they're still looking. It's a place where you can't give up. But seeing those almost-empty tents makes my heart stutter. Everything looks done. Over.

I try to make sense of what I'm seeing. Which building was

where? It's so hard to distinguish anything beyond the piles of concrete and broken walls.

I push on with purpose. Me and my crusty sweatshirt and my water bottle and Charlie's journal. I survey the rubble, thinking it makes me look important. Like I'm supposed to be here. But when I take one step too many, I'm stopped by a shout.

"You can't go there!" The voice is loud and bold and feels like it's literally pushing down on my shoulders to keep me from taking another step.

I turn to see a big man with a big dog. He's wearing a bright orange vest and holding something that kind of looks like a laptop with a handle on it. A portable radar detector. I've seen them on TV. It senses heartbeats and breathing. The dog pads around him, sniffing at the cracks and crevices. Like the dog that found me.

I take another step forward.

"I said stop."

He's in front of me now.

"My mom worked here," I say. "I have to find her." I lift my chin, daring him to stop me.

"You can't find your mom?" His voice is calmer. Softer. Kinder.

There's something about his kindness that makes me want to cry. But I will not break. I will not.

"No." I straighten my shoulders. "And I'm sick of people telling me to sit and wait."

He nods. "Understandable."

The dog brushes past his leg. The man instinctively runs his hand across its head as it goes. It stops at my feet. Sniffs. Won't move on. It presses its nose to my hand. Nuzzles. I remember the press of a dog's wet nose finding me in front of the laundromat. The shouts. *Stay with me.*

"Are you sure she was in the building when The Big One hit?" he asks.

"Pretty sure."

I look at the rubble. Take in the mess. Weigh the risk. Count the chances.

"Were there survivors here?"

"There were. We actually pulled two people out late last night." He looks like he's remembering. "Two women."

Two women. Last night. "They were alive?"

"They were critical."

"Where are they now?"

"We sent them by medevac to SHC Med."

"Where is that? How do I get there?"

"It's about twenty minutes south. On a good day. And . . ." He looks around. "This isn't exactly a good day."

I stare at the ground. I've already come so far from the other direction. My legs can barely hold me up anymore. How am I supposed to get somewhere else?

"Can you take me?"

He draws in a breath. "I'm not supposed to do stuff like that."

I sink. Sit. The dog sits down next to me. Licks my hand. I close my eyes. Lift my face to the sun. Try to collect myself. I remember that sliver of light through the rubble and the way it led me from day to night and day again. I open my eyes. Look right at him. The dog sniffs at my hand. Pulls at the edge of my sweatshirt. Whimpers.

The man looks at me closely. Closer. He shakes his head like he's clearing it.

"No way," he says.

"What?"

"Were you at . . . a laundromat?"

I freeze. I am frozen. "Yes."

"No."

"Yes." I watch him. Because now I know. "It was you."

"It was me." He shakes his head again like he can't believe how small and real and astonishing the world actually is. "I'm so glad you're okay. We don't always know if the people we help end up okay."

I clench my fists. Look at him as my eyes fill with tears. "I'm not okay. I'm breaking. I need to find my mom. She's all I have."

He looks around. Watches the dog. Stares at the emptiness. Scratches his head. "Wait here."

He walks up and over and through the wreckage to a tent in the distance. His big boots thump against the ground as he goes. The same way they did when he carried me out of the rubble. I remember his big hands and his calm voice.

Stay with me, he'd said. *Stay.*

I want to say the same thing to him right now. *Stay with me. Don't leave me to figure this out alone.* Because seeing him, someone familiar after so many strangers, makes me feel like he's someone I know.

Someone I'm meant to know.

Like Charlie. And Nurse Cathy.

The man comes back. Offers his hand to help me up.

I take it.

His grip is instantly comforting.

"Come with me," he says. "I'm Mitchell. I think I can help."

CHAPTER FORTY-THREE

12:25 P.M.

THE INSIDE OF THE TENT MITCHELL TAKES me to is filled with food and water and phones and computers. And people doing things. Helping. Organizing. It's a finely tuned machine in the middle of chaos.

"How are you running all of this?" I ask.

"FEMA. We're set up for search and rescue and triage. And those emergency cell towers make communication possible by phone and computer."

"Your phones *work*?"

"That's why I brought you here," Mitchell says as his dog sniffs at my feet. "Call your mom."

"I thought none of this stuff was working. Like anywhere."

"Until last night, it wasn't. More towers went up this morning. Phones are finally getting reception. Go ahead. Try."

I can barely dial because my hands are shaking. What if I call my mom and she doesn't answer? What if I get that old-timey ring again? I feel like I'm being set up for failure here. But on the second ring someone answers. A man. I almost hang up, convinced my shaky fingers dialed the wrong number. Or the temporary phone towers are making wires cross.

"Mom? I'm looking for my mom."

"Ruby, is that you?" The voice crackles through the line. "Where are you? Are you okay?"

I recognize him this time.

"Coach? Where are you? Are you with my mom? Is she okay?"

"Where are *you* right now?"

My words come out in a rush. Telling him how I got here. About the hospital. The van. The devastation at my mom's office. The tent. Mitchell.

"Don't move. I'll come to you."

"Is my mom there? Are you both coming?"

But he's already hung up.

Mitchell assures me it's the unreliable reception, but I worry it's something more. That Coach is coming because my mom can't. Why did he answer her phone? Why didn't he reassure me that she's okay?

CHAPTER FORTY-FOUR

1:21 P.M.

I DOWN THE REST OF MY WATER AND REFUSE a browned banana while I wait for Coach to arrive. My stomach coils. Helpless.

There's a chair and a blanket and people who are okay with letting me sit here. Someone from the triage tent unwraps my arm bandage, checks my wound, reapplies clean gauze. I'm glad when he tells me it's healing okay. No sign of infection. But I also want to tell him to help someone else instead of me. Or take to the streets like Ava and Luke. He could be busy finding people who are trapped like I was instead of changing out my gauze. Checking on me doesn't matter right now. My mom is the only thing that matters.

Where is she? Is she okay?

It's an eternity before I see Coach, but when I finally do, I run to him. I'm so relieved to see him wearing his team sweatshirt and his Pacific Shore High School hat as if he were standing on the pool deck before practice instead of outside a triage tent. His clothes are clean, like he's been someplace safe. Like he can keep me safe. Like he'll protect me. How did I not realize that until now? I fall against him. Everything hits me at once. How long I've been alone. How I had to claw my way out of the rubble and fight for my life in the hospital. How I had to escape this morning and walk so far to find help. The thoughts make me crumble. I go down like the walls of the laundromat until I'm a heap on the ground. Bent over. Bunched up. A heaving mass of sobs and relief. Coach holds me up. Tucks me in. Lets me cry.

"I've been looking everywhere for you," he says.

"Where's my mom? I called her phone from the hospital. I couldn't get through."

"Nobody could. But she refused to let go of her phone."

"But where is she now? Why isn't she here?"

"She's okay, but she's in a hospital. She has some injuries. They're serious, but she's going to be okay."

"Take me to her."

"That's why I'm here."

HERE

I am here.
   I am feet on the pavement.
   I am blood in my veins.
   I am muscles and nerves,
      and sinew and bones.
   I am fingers that wield pens like swords.
   I am legs that kick through doors.
   I am today.
   I am tomorrow.
   I am toes in the sand.
   I am air in my lungs.
   I am a walk in the woods.
   I am a boat on the ocean.
   I am push.
   I am pull.
   I am real.

   I am here.

CHAPTER FORTY-FIVE

3:33 P.M.

INSIDE THE HOSPITAL, THERE'S A DESK AND there's a person. She has a list and she has names. She can say who's here. And who isn't.

Coach walks over to her. Smiles. He pulls something from his pocket. He has credentials. A badge. Something official. Something that says he can be here.

I stand.

I shift.

I need them to hurry. I need to see my mom now.

Coach motions me over. He hands me a pen and points to a line on a piece of paper. I sign my name. Then we write our names on stickers that we fasten to our chests.

The woman at the desk points straight ahead and we walk that way. Down a hallway and to a door. Coach says something else to somebody there. They open the door.

And there she is. My mom.

She is tubes and beeps and bruises. Broken. Bundled. But she is also arms and legs. She is here and now. She is breath and air. I can see things aren't perfect. I want her to move but she won't. She can't. It's clear she has to heal.

She isn't awake.

But she is alive.

My old fear creeps in. *Hospitals are where people go to die.* Is this how my mom felt when she came to see my dad? Am I going to have to say goodbye to her and watch someone sign papers to let her go?

Stop. I shake my head. This is where she needs to be. This is where people can help her. Being here is her best chance at getting better. The same way I did. There are Nurse Cathys and Doctor Patels here. People who can help. People who can heal.

Behind me the doctor explains that my mom has a concussion and some internal injuries. Broken bones. Dehydration. An ambulance brought her here earlier this week. He tells me how my mom was trapped. Buried. Stuck. Crushed. Just like I was. And Charlie. But she made it out.

"She's going to be okay," the doctor assures me. "She just needs time."

Coach braces his hand on my shaking shoulder. Talks to me in his calm voice.

"Go see her," he says. "She needs you."

DAY NINE

SATURDAY

CHAPTER FORTY-SIX

9:09 A.M.

I HAVE A CRICK IN MY NECK FROM SLEEPING on the floor next to my mom's hospital bed, but I wouldn't want to be anywhere else. Not that I have anywhere else to go. I hear a rustling. Imagine the gentle smoothing back of my hair.

I look up. See my mom's eyes flutter. Focus.

She's here.

The smell of her. The softness.

I reach out to touch her. To know she's real. I stand up so I can reach her. My hands hold her cheeks like a mug of hot tea. The vision of her blurs through the tears in my eyes. Like she's swimming in me. I'm swimming in her.

"Ruby." Her own eyes go blurry with tears. "Oh, Ruby. I was so afraid I'd never find you." She looks at me. At this bed. At this room. At how serious it all is. At how close something bad seemed. "I was so afraid I'd lose you, too."

"Never." She has loved me fiercely, but been too afraid to let anyone in since my dad. Until Coach. Because loving too hard meant accepting the risk of losing it.

"Are you okay?" she asks. "Where have you been?"

"I was hurt. I was in the hospital."

She gasps. Reaches out for a hug. I go to her and she pulls me in. "The hospital? This hospital?"

"A different one."

"How did you get there? Who took care of you? How did you get here?" Her voice is muffled against my hair.

I tell her everything. About the rubble. About Charlie. My rescue. Nurse Cathy. Luke and Ava. "But I'm okay."

"Ruby," she says, "you were so mad at me—"

I lean back. Look her in the eye. "Mom, I'm so sorry. I should've listened. I should've explained how I was feeling. I think you're brave. It must be scary to fall in love after you fell in love once and lost everything."

"Oh, sweet girl. I didn't lose everything. I got you." She tears up. Puts her hand to my cheek. "I was so afraid I wouldn't find you again."

"I found Coach," I say.

"We found each other," he says.

I can see the peace on my mom's face. Like she has all she needs right here right now. And I can see how much Coach cares. About my mom. About me. And I'm okay with that. I'm okay if he's in our living room on Sundays and on our couch on Christmas. I'm okay if he's in our house and in our lives. I'm okay if he comes with my mom to drop me off at college and meet at the airport when I fly home in the summertime.

I'm okay.

We're okay.

I have only a little bit of time left before I leave for college. I don't want to spend that time fighting with the people I love. I don't want to fight with my mom and I don't want to fight with Leo. I don't want to fight with Mila, either. I hope I get a chance to tell her that.

I wish Charlie would've had the chance to do the same with his parents.

I need to focus on spending the time I have with the people I love because I'm meant to go away soon. To move on. And after that, my mom is meant to be here with Coach.

MOVING ON

L ast fall, my mom and I went on a college tour. It was about what I'd expected: an enthusiastic student, currently enrolled, walked us around campus, pointing out landmarks and bestowing us with breathless stats of everything the school had to offer.

I could see myself there.

Walking along the pathways strewn with the bright reds and oranges of fallen autumn leaves.

I could see myself living in the sleek and modern dorm building and eating in the dining hall.

I could see myself crossing campus to get to the pool, before the sun came up, for a morning workout. And heading to class afterward with wet hair and coffee.

I could see myself sitting in the back row of a lecture hall for an English literature class or in the front row of a biology lab.

I could see everything in such clear focus that my body buzzed with the excitement of it all.

We met the water polo coach, who seemed enthusiastic about my high school athletic career. They told me to stay in touch and that they'd try to catch one of my games in the upcoming season.

I was so taken with the campus, with the vibe and the energy and the students being free and on their own.

"Can I get a sweatshirt?" I asked my mom. "From the student store?"

"Sure."

At the store, we sifted through sweatshirts, so many different designs for one college, and picked out one that felt classic. Timeless. I had the clerk at the register cut the tag off for me so I could wear it home.

When we got back to the car, my mom was slow to start the engine. She simply sat and looked out the window at the crowded parking lot. At the buildings in the distance. And the students walking by.

I was sold.

Cal was where I wanted to be.

My mom gripped the steering wheel, still not starting the car.

"Mom?" I asked. "Are we going to sit here all day?"

When I looked closer, I saw that her eyes were shiny. Her quiet took over the car. It was too much. Too silent.

"Mom?" I said again.

She swiped at her eyes. "Yeah. Yes."

"What's wrong?" I said.

"Nothing."

She started the car. It grumbled. Like it didn't want to leave, either.

My mom looked over her shoulder, ready to back out, but settled her gaze on me as the car idled in its parking space. I noticed a student in a beat-up maroon Toyota waiting for our spot, their blinker flashing in order to claim it.

My mom pressed the palm of her hand to my cheek and said, "All your life, I've been working on preparing you to be ready to go. But maybe I should've been preparing myself." Her voice faltered. Her lip wobbled. "You're leaving. And I won't be coming with you."

"Mom—"

"It's okay, Ruby. It's how things are meant to be. I love you and I know you're going to be okay. And I'm going to be, too. But I'll miss you a lot and I'm going to be a little sad. What can I say? I'm a mom. It's what I do."

"I'll miss you, too. I will."

She smiled. "Oh, sweet girl, no, you won't. You won't have time to miss me. But that's okay."

The driver of the maroon Toyota honked their horn, making my mom and me jump in our seats.

My mom checked her eye makeup in the rearview mirror, swiped at the black smudge of mascara that had leaked from her lashes. And then she put the car in reverse and backed out. We didn't say anything else as we drove out of the lot and onto the road toward home.

Quiet.

Together.

CHAPTER FORTY-SEVEN

11:45 A.M.

COACH TURNS HIS CAR ONTO MY STREET.
There have been stories of people looting and squatting at damaged and abandoned homes, so my mom sent Coach and me to not only see if our house is still standing, but to retrieve her Parental Box of Important Papers along with some other must-haves. I tick off the houses as we go. The Richardsons. The Chens. The Storeys. The young hipster couple with the year-round Christmas lights. Nobody is walking dogs or riding bikes or bringing in their groceries in reusable Trader Joe's bags.

Nobody is here.

Nothing is normal.

Our house is literally sagging sideways. Off-kilter. Like some suburban Leaning Tower of Pisa. And the magnolia tree from our front yard has fallen straight across the driveway. Coach pulls to the curb and I'm out of the car before he's even put it in park.

"Stop!" Coach yells. "It might not be safe to go inside!"

I don't care. I turn the knob of the front door, somehow expecting it to swing open even though we always lock our doors, but the dead bolt is in place just as my mom would've left it when she went to work the day of the earthquake. I jiggle the doorknob again, like I can unlock it by sheer force of will.

"Slow down. We need to be careful," Coach says.

I twist the knob again. Try to break it. Kick the wood. Pound with my fist. All of these things make my whole body hurt. I push past Coach to kneel down and sift through the dirt and flowers by the front door, trying to unearth our hidden key. I work around the broken remnants of terra-cotta flowerpots, slicing my finger on one of them. I don't stop to check the cut. I don't even care. Soil pushes up underneath my fingernails as I tear the garden apart. I finally find the key and turn it in the lock. I push the door open with such force it bounces against the wall of the entryway and swings back in Coach's face. He stops it with an outstretched arm.

Inside there's nothing. Only silence. And the remnants of what was.

Pictures have fallen off the walls, their frames shattered. I lunge forward as broken shards of glass crunch underneath the bright white sneakers Nurse Cathy gave me at the hospital. Coach puts his arm across me like he's stopped short at a stoplight and wants to protect me from hurtling through the windshield.

"Goddammit," Coach says, making me wait while he gingerly takes a step forward. "Hold on, Ruby. This is serious."

I stand still for him and look around.

I want this house to feel like home. For my mom to emerge from the kitchen to ask about my day. For Leo to be sitting next to me on the couch, our hands in a bowl of popcorn, the movie too loud. All the little things I've taken for granted.

But home is broken.

The shelves have toppled over. The books are spread across the living room like bodies. Spines twisted. Pages bent.

Like Charlie in the rubble.

Securing our bookshelves was one of those weekend projects my mom kept talking about but never did. One of those things you're supposed to do to be earthquake ready, but then a weekend matinee or sleeping in or a sunny day at the beach sounds better.

I slowly crunch my way through the carnage to get to the kitchen. Pantry doors have been flung wide open. Pots and pans, dishes, coffee mugs, and glass jars of spaghetti sauce have broken free, the sauce leaving smears of red, chunky liquid across the white tile floor.

I'm exhausted. It's too much. I crumble to the floor and push a cabinet door shut so I can lean against it for support.

"Mom's box of papers is upstairs, in her closet, on the top shelf," I tell Coach. "It's probably on the floor now."

"Let me go first and make sure it's safe up there."

"I want to get some of my stuff. Better clothes, too. And something for my mom to change into when she's released."

Coach nods.

I curl into myself after he goes. Hold my breath. Hold my stomach. Stuff my feelings in. Because we don't have a house. We don't have a home.

We just have silence.

Like when Charlie went quiet.

Charlie.

Coach comes back to the kitchen minutes later.

"About the same up there as here," he says.

"Can I go up to change clothes and pack a backpack?"

"Get enough clothes for you and your mom. You won't be coming back here. You two will stay with me. My house had minimal damage." Coach commutes to work, and his town didn't get hit as hard as ours did.

I unearth my team duffel bag from the mess of clothes on my closet floor and shove jeans and sweats and shirts and underwear inside. A toothbrush. Toothpaste. Tampons. Shampoo. I go to my mom's room and do the same.

On the way out, my eye catches on a photo. One of her and my dad in Italy. Laughing on the beach with sun-streaked hair. I pull it loose from the broken frame and shove it into my bag.

"I'm ready," I say. Coach holds the door open for me, grabs my bag and slings it over his shoulder. I stop short at the threshold. Look him in the eye.

"Wait. Is this going to be weird? My mom and me living with you?"

"I don't want it to be weird. I can make it not weird if you can."

That makes me laugh, and I guess I'm lucky. At least I like Coach. And respect him. And he is funny when he wants to be.

"Let's go," Coach says. "I'm sure your mom is missing you since she just got you back."

CHAPTER FORTY-EIGHT

2:50 P.M.

IN THE DIM LIGHT OF THE HOSPITAL ROOM, I sift through Charlie's journal while my mom sleeps. I turn to the last filled page, curious to know what he was writing when I watched him at the laundromat. Across the top, underlined, he'd written, *What I Wish I Could Say to Mom and Dad.*

Dear Mom and Dad,

I want to tell you my story. In my words.

It's a detailed account about what happened that night at the fraternity house. The words are the same ones he'd used to tell me. About Jason. The frat house. The defibrillator. The guilt.

I want you to understand that I'm scared and I'm sad and I really need my parents right now.

The words stop. Like he had more to say and didn't know how to say it.

And then, abruptly in the middle of the page, not connected at all, but in the same color pen, it says:

More later. A cute girl just walked into the laundromat and I bet she wants me to buy her beer. We'll see if I can restrain myself from lecturing her. She looks smart enough to know better.

So he knew why I was there all along? And he was just waiting for me to say something? I laugh out loud.

Charlie.

I close his journal and hug it to my chest.

———

Later, Coach tells me about what happened on the pool deck when the earthquake hit. How it was the middle of practice. How he was worried about my not being there and what he would tell my mom.

"Iris didn't make it," he says.

I suck in a breath. Shake my head. "No."

"I was waiting to tell you. I wanted you to see your mom first and to know she was okay and you both had a safe place to stay."

My eyes tear. I've known Iris since kindergarten. After me, Iris was the best at standing up to Mila.

Mila.

"But the rest of my friends are okay? Thea and Juliette?" *What about Mila? Where is she?*

Coach nods. "Thea and Juliette are fine."

"Have you heard anything about Mila?"

"I haven't. I wish I had, though."

"I don't know if you've noticed, but we haven't really been speaking to each other."

"I noticed." He leans forward in his chair.

"I tried to talk to her. I wanted her to get help, but I'm not trained in that sort of thing. For all I know, I said the wrong thing."

"You talked to her from a place of concern. You wanted her to get help because you care about her." He shrugs. "That sounds about right to me. Sometimes we can only do the best we know how to do at the time. And it sounds like you did that."

"That's good advice." I wish Charlie were here so I could tell it to him. He did the best he knew how to do at the time with Jason.

Coach continues. "That was some pretty heavy stuff that went down with Mila. And she was probably angry at first. At you and me. Not because we are to blame for her choices, but because it was easier to blame someone else instead of herself."

"Can I ask you something?"

"Of course."

"Did you give me more playing time because of my mom? Did you feel like you had to?"

His brows scrunch. He looks like I slapped him in the face. "Why would you think that?"

"Mila said it."

"Ah." He really looks at me. "And no."

"I wanted to quit. I didn't want special treatment."

"I would've been disappointed in you if you'd quit, but I

would've been more disappointed in myself. I would've failed you as a coach." He shakes his head. "You get game time because you're my number one offensive player, Ruby. Period."

"Okay. I believe you."

"Good. And Ruby?"

"Yeah."

"You can't blame yourself for what happened to Mila." Coach sounds like me talking to Charlie in the rubble. "You can't force her to get help. She has to want it for herself. That wasn't her first offense, you know? She was suspended for a few days in October for something similar."

"She was?"

"Yes. She didn't tell you?"

"No."

But I suddenly remember those October days. She'd told us her mom was making her visit a sick aunt in Palm Springs. It was the middle of the week and it seemed weird to me that they couldn't wait until the weekend. The sad part is they'd actually gone. And probably sat by the pool and ordered room service, thankful for the excuse to have a minivacation. One offense was suspension. A second offense gave the school no other choice but to expel her.

And still, she hadn't wanted help.

I know how hard it is to ask for help. To admit that you need it. I hope Mila is strong enough to see it now. Because if this last week has taught me anything, it's that I can't do everything on my own. Asking for help got me here. It's how I got better in the hospital and how I found my mom. Asking for help doesn't make people weak. It makes them strong.

"I think there's a chance Mila's ready for help," Coach says. "Sometimes you have to get to the worst place before you can climb back out."

"That makes sense." Mila lost everything. Her team. Her college water polo dreams. Her school. Her friends. "I just want her to be okay."

"So do I."

My mom stirs. Opens her eyes. Sees us whispering, heads close together, trying not to wake her.

"What did I miss?" she says.

"Only a little coach-and-player talk," Coach says.

"You two. All water polo all the time."

Coach walks to her. Squeezes her hand. "You hungry? Thirsty? What can I get you?"

"Water would be great. If you can find it."

"I will."

He hands me his phone as he goes. "I've got all my players in my contacts. Even Mila. Why don't you go ahead and give it a try?"

"Thanks."

"Good luck."

My mom rolls to her side to see me better when he's gone. She winces.

"How's the pain?" I ask.

"It hurts enough to hurt."

"I know what you mean. More than you know."

"I wish you didn't."

In an instant I'm there again. In the cold and the dark. In the tiny coffin space of the laundromat with Charlie not breathing next to me. "Were you scared?"

"I was terrified. But not just for me. I was worried about you." She sniffs. "There were only a few of us in the office at the time. We didn't all make it. And my head . . . I knew something was seriously wrong. It was a concussion. I was afraid to sleep."

"Yeah. Charlie and I tried to take turns sleeping."

"That was smart."

"I feel like I went through this thing that nobody else could possibly understand. But you actually do. You were trapped like I was."

"And now I have to get better like you did."

"That sounds mildly optimistic."

She smiles and her eyes crinkle. "I try."

"I know."

CHAPTER FORTY-NINE

3:52 P.M.

IT TAKES A WHILE, BUT I FINALLY GET through to Thea. She picks up on the first ring and I tell her it's me, not Coach.

"Oh my god! Ruby! Where the hell have you been?"

"Is there any way you can get to SHC Med? My mom's here. I can tell you everything, but I don't want to suck up what's left of Coach's phone charge."

An hour later, Thea and Juliette arrive at the hospital.

Mila trails behind them, her arm in a cast. I hope it says something that she's here. That maybe we'll be okay after all.

It doesn't look right to see all of them without Iris.

I collide into a group hug with Thea and Juliette while Mila hangs back. I look at her and she shrugs. I pull her in, too. The four of us hang on tight, everyone crying. We cry about the fact that we're here and Iris isn't.

Once we collect ourselves, we sit and my friends inundate me with questions. Thea lets me use her phone to text Leo because she has him in her contacts and Coach doesn't. My text won't go through and I have to keep trying. My friends listen while I tell them about Charlie. And being trapped.

"Unreal," Juliette says, shaking her head.

They tell me what happened at the pool when the earthquake hit. How Coach knew what to do and how he kept them safe.

"He tried so hard to save Iris," Thea says, her voice catching, like she's seeing it all flash in front of her again.

The same way I keep flashing to the rubble. And my hospital bed. And the stairwell. I keep seeing it. I always will.

"Coach was pretty calm, but he was totally worried about you," Juliette says. "Grilling all of us about where you were. Like he was personally responsible for your safety."

"He'd do that for any of us," I say.

"He took care of Iris like she was his own kid," Thea says.

"See? It's not just me." I look at Mila. "Despite what you want to think about me getting special treatment or whatever."

"I shouldn't have said that. It was a messed-up thing to say."

"You've said a lot of messed-up things," I tell her.

"I know. I'm sorry."

"Oh, man, Iris would've loved this," Thea says. "The two of you making up."

And then we're all crying again. For the loss of our friend—and life as we knew it.

Until Thea's phone dings.

"Oh! It's Leo!" She holds the phone up for me to see the text on the screen.

I'll be there as fast as I can.

"He's on his way," I say, a smile taking over my face as my body floods with relief. Leo is okay. I'm going to see him. I'm going to be able to hug him and hold him and be held by him. I'm so thankful.

"I'm starving," Juliette says.

I dig into my pocket. Rip open a protein bar and divide it into even squares. We chew slowly, and I try to imagine that the tasteless, sticky lump in my mouth is a slice of pizza instead.

But then Mila says, "This is disgusting." And we all bust out laughing.

"It's the worst," I admit.

"When will we have real food again?" Thea whimpers.

"When will we have water polo practice again?" Juliette says. "Is our season just over?"

"Coach'll find a way," I say.

Mila sits quietly next to me. "Wish I could be there," she finally says. She turns to me. "I haven't told anyone yet, but I decided to enter treatment. This whole week has been, I don't know, life-changing, right? For everyone. I've had a lot of time to think and . . . I just . . . I don't want to die." She swipes at her eyes.

"I don't want you to die, either." I pull her into a hug. "And

I don't want to fight with you anymore. I miss my best friend. The one who always had my back. The one who made a pact with me when we were ten years old and the only two girls on a team of boys."

"I'm going to try to do better," she mumbles into my shoulder. "I need to get help. And it's going to be hard."

"I'm here if you need me."

"We all are," Thea says.

"Thanks," says Mila. "It won't be easy. I'm sure I'll need all of you."

And she's right. It won't be easy. Rehab is hard work. She might slip. Stumble. But all I can hope is that she'll keep trying. She has to try every day.

We hang out a while longer, going floor-to-floor to find something left in a vending machine while swapping our best Iris stories. I'm grateful for the simplicity of the moment. And for the loyalty of my friends.

"Thank you for coming all this way," I say.

"We had to see you," Thea says.

"Unfortunately, I think we have to head out now," Juliette says. "It's getting dark, and there's a curfew at the shelter."

"Totally get it," I say. "I'll find my way to you next time."

We hug again. Promise we'll keep tabs on one another. Coach comes out of my mom's room to say goodbye. Tells my friends to be safe. And they've got his number if they need him. Or me.

After they go, Coach heads off to ask for something from the nurse's station.

And then I wait.

When Leo arrives, he reaches out. Pulls me in. I sink.

I fall completely and wholly into the familiar safety of him. He draws me in. Tighter. Closer. Like he can't believe it's really me. I know exactly how he feels. And then he pulls back. Touches my face. Making sure I'm here and true. He runs his fingertip over the stitches on my arm. His brow twists with worry.

"I was freaking out, Ruby."

"I know. Me too."

He knots his fingers with mine. Kisses each of my knuckles. "I was so bummed about what I said the other day. And how it made you feel. That was the last time we were together. That was the last time I saw you."

And then I remember what he said about my hands and how upset I got. It seemed like such a big deal when it happened. It doesn't matter now, but this is what Leo has been worrying about. This wish for different last words. I know how awful that must've been, because it's the same way I've been wishing my last conversation with my mom hadn't been about how she'd ruined my life. We remember the last things we say to people. It's what was on Charlie's mind. Maybe even Mila's. We all want to have a chance to go back and make things right again, but we don't all get that chance.

But right now Leo does.

And I do.

We're lucky.

I can say the things I want to say to him. The things I need to say.

"I love you." I lean in. Kiss him. Push my fingers through his curly hair to pull him closer. I put every ounce of reassurance I can into this moment. Life can change in an instant. It's important to let the ones you love know how you feel. "It's okay. I'm okay. I love you. We're okay."

FOUR MONTHS LATER . . .

I KNOCK ON THE HEAVY WOOD DOOR. IT took a lot to find this place. I remembered Charlie saying his brother worked at the Apple Store at the mall so I started my research there. Talking to Charlie's brother led me to here: a nondescript rental home right off the freeway.

I clutch Charlie's journal to my chest, a little sad to let it go. When I read his words, I could hear him. So giving them up is almost like letting him go all over again.

The door opens and a woman about my mom's age studies me. She has light hair, almost white at the tips, and bright blue eyes. I try to see Charlie in her. There are pieces of him. I can tell.

"Can I help you?" she asks.

I clear my throat. "I'm Ruby. I was at the laundromat with Charlie."

She pulls her hand to her chest. "Oh, my goodness."

I hold the journal out to her. "These are Charlie's words. You should know them. They're important."

She reaches for the journal. She's shaking. And I realize how important this is. I'm giving her a piece of her son. Something else she can have to remember him by. To know him in a way she'd never realized. My heart breaks even more when I acknowledge Charlie won't ever get the chance to be with his mom and dad again, to remind them love is what matters, not grades and schools and disagreements. Family is worth fighting for. Love is worth fighting for.

She runs her hand along the front of the journal, letting her fingers linger over the raised gold letters of his name. When she looks at me again, her eyes are shiny with tears. A mixture of happy and sad.

"Thank you," she says. "This is such a gift."

"Charlie was a gift to me. I'm glad I got to know him."

"You were at the laundromat with him?"

"I was. I think a part of me will always be there."

And it's true. I'm always there in the rubble. In the cold and the dust with that tiny spray of light coming through the crack above my head. Before then, I'd always thought of aftershocks as the literal rumblings the ground made after an earthquake, but they're something different to me now. Aftershocks are the part that stays forever, rolling in when you're unprepared, triggered by something big and undeniable or small and unexpected. Aftershocks are PTSD, survivor's guilt, and grief. Aftershocks are what wakes me up in a cold sweat in the middle of the night, convincing me I'm still there, in the rubble with Charlie. Aftershocks are why I and pretty much everyone else I know go to therapy.

"I can only imagine," she says, her voice drifting like she's trying to be there with Charlie. Like she wants to. Because she's his mom. "I owe you a thank-you."

"He told me stuff. About his life. And what happened," I say.

His mom smiles. But it doesn't reach her eyes. "Leave it to Charlie to share everything with a stranger."

"We weren't strangers. Maybe at first, but not in the end."

"Right." She shakes her head, clearing it. "Of course not. You wouldn't be strangers after what you went through together."

"It's not just that." I want to make it as clear as I can. "He was kind to me. And he was brave. He was a good person and he had beautiful dreams. You should be proud of the son you raised."

Charlie was a big heart in a small space.

I was lucky to have known him.

"Thank you," she says. "Thank you for coming all this way. For finding me so I could have this." She pulls the journal to her chest so much like I did.

"You'll see who he was in his words." I point to the journal. "There are poems in there. And stories. And truth. I hope you'll love reading it. I loved reading it."

"I know I will." She shakes her head and sniffs as her tears fall freely. "Ruby"—she sucks in a breath—"can you do one more thing for me? Can you promise to go live a big and beautiful life and do all the things Charlie won't get to do?"

"I will."

I mean it.

As I turn to go, she mumbles something I don't make out the first time. And then she says it again. "Water polo." Then, "Ruby! Wait! You're the water polo player? You play water polo?"

I turn back around. "Yes, I play water polo." My sweatshirt kind of gives it away.

"Oh, my goodness!" She flaps her hands in excitement. "Wait here. I have something . . . I think it might be yours. Can you wait a minute?"

"Sure."

She rushes back into the house and returns to me a moment later.

"I think this belongs to you." She holds up my championship ring. The ring I spun around and around my finger while Charlie told me why I should be proud of it. And then he promised to keep it safe for me.

"But I wanted Charlie to have it."

"That is so sweet of you. But it doesn't feel right. You need to hold on to it."

I remember how Charlie said his mom always made decisions for him. I guess this is another one of them. I want to force her to keep it, but then I realize there isn't any point to Charlie's mom having my ring. Because if she has it, it means he's not wearing it anymore. But if it's on my finger, it will be a reminder of him. Of my friend. I take it from her and slip it back on my own finger, where it belongs.

"Thank you."

"No, Ruby. Thank *you*."

She shuts the door behind me and I listen to the lock click into place as I go.

"Let's go to the beach," Mila says when I'm back in the car. "I need to see the ocean today."

"Me too."

We wind our way through reopened roads and park near the pier. I follow Mila through the sand, letting it sift between my toes, reminding me how lucky I am to still be able to savor the small things like this. To appreciate how important they are, too.

We sit down and watch the ocean. Listen to the steady rhythm of the waves going in and out. Constant and reassuring like a heartbeat. And then I lie back. Feel the warm sun on my face. I remember Charlie in the rubble, telling me to close my eyes and imagine someplace better than where we were. To let all of my senses take over. I close my eyes again now. I imagine his voice in my head.

Do you feel that, Ruby? Do you smell it? You're here. You're home.

Additional Resources

For more information on earthquake safety and preparedness, visit FEMA at fema.gov, the American Red Cross at redcross.org, and the Great ShakeOut at shakeout.org.

If you think you or someone you care about may need help with substance abuse, contact the Substance Abuse and Mental Health Services Administration (SAMHSA) at samhsa.gov or 1-800-662-HELP (4357).

Acknowledgments

Kate Testerman, my wonderful agent at KT Literary, thank you for always trusting and believing in this book. Your endless optimism is everything an author could hope for and I'm so grateful for you.

Maggie Lehrman, my incredible editor at Amulet, thank you for loving Ruby as much as I do and helping to make her story fuller and richer. I feel so lucky to have worked with you.

Neil Swaab and Hana Nakamura, thank you for a stunning and perfect cover for *Aftershocks*. And to the entire team at Amulet, thank you for all you've done, every step of the way, to bring this book into the world. I'm truly honored.

Elise Robins and Stacy Wise, my amazing critique partners, thank you for always being my first readers and freshest eyes. We've come so far since our inaugural meeting so many years ago and I'm so proud of us.

Shannon Parker, with your keen eye and stellar notes, thank you for helping make sense of this book when it needed it the most. Charlie wouldn't be Charlie without you.

My friends in the YA community who are always there for me: Shea Ernshaw, Jeff Garvin, Kerry Kletter, Amy Spalding, Kali Wallace, and Darcy Woods, thank you for always being a text or phone call away on top of being the amazing people you are.

Jim Laing, thank you for answering my emergency medical

questions at a moment's notice. You came through when Ruby and I needed you most.

Lee Gjertsen Malone, thank you for taking the time to share your knowledge of the American Red Cross and disaster relief. Your input was valuable beyond words.

My mom and brother, thank you for your constant support and enthusiasm.

And finally, Jon and Kai, you are the very best part of my life. Thank you. I love you.

About the Author

Marisa Reichardt is the author of *Underwater* and *Aftershocks*. She lives in Southern California and can usually be found huddled over her laptop in a coffeehouse or swimming in the ocean.